The Potter's Wheel

The Potter's Wheel

By

Billie Houston

Desert Breeze Publishing, Inc.
27305 W. Live Oak Rd #424
Castaic, CA 91384

http://www.DesertBreezePublishing.com

ISBN 13: 978-1-68294-950-4

Published in the United States of America
Publish Date: April 2016

Editor-In-Chief: Gail R. Delaney
Editor: Christy Dyer
Marketing Director: Jenifer Ranieri
Cover Artist: Carol Fiorillo

Dedication and Acknowledgment

For the members of my Greatest Generation Bible Class. I was a stranger and you took me in.

Other Books By Billie Houston

John Jacob Worthington Jones

Chapter One

Dallas, Texas,
Train Terminal
Saturday Morning
April 7th, 1917

Ruth Garland lifted her travel skirt with one hand, grasped her satchel with the other, and put one foot on the first step upward. "Is this the train to Waco?"

The conductor nodded. "Yes, Ma'am, it is." He placed his hand under her elbow and gave her a boost. "Move along, please."

Ruth located the economy coach and found a seat. She was not about to pay two dollars for a first class ticket to Waco when she could ride economy for a dollar and fifty cents. She moved to a seat by the window and pushed her satchel under it.

The coach filled rapidly. Most of the passengers were men. Some were accompanied by women. A few had children with them. Maybe she made a mistake deciding to travel alone.

No one noticed she was alone. No one noticed her, period. An atmosphere of expectancy stirred the air.

A young woman appeared beside her. "Is this seat taken?"

Ruth welcomed the sight of another young female traveling alone. Well, almost alone, she had a child with her. "No, please sit down."

The woman sat, put her paper bag under her seat, and lifted the child into her lap. "My name is Flossie Johnson, and this is my daughter, Ruby." Her smile was engaging. "Are you going far?"

Ruth returned her smile. "My name is Ruth Garland. I'm going to Waco."

"You will be getting off before I do. I'm going all the way to Austin." Flossie leaned back and settled into a more comfortable position.

With a jerk and a mighty groan, the train pulled from the station, huffing and puffing and blowing smoke like an angry dragon.

The conductor came down the aisle, holding onto seat backs to keep his balance, as he called, "Tickets, tickets, please."

Ruth hunted through her satchel, found her purse, and had her ticket ready when he stopped to collect it.

"You will change trains in Corsicana," he told her, as he punched her ticket. "You have a two-hour and thirty minute layover there."

A scowl clouded the conductor's face when he examined Flossie's ticket. "You have no ticket for your child. That means you cannot put her in a seat beside you, even if it's empty, and don't let her annoy other passengers. Is that understood?" He punched her ticket, and gave it back to her.

Flossie took the ticket, dropped her head and blushed. "Yes, sir."

Ruth was furious. "Sir, and I use the term loosely, you have insulted my friend. Apologize."

The conductor turned his scowling gaze toward Ruth. "We have rules here, Ma'am. It is my duty to convey them to passengers who might break them."

"*Might* break them?" Ruth questioned.

Flossie interrupted, "It's all right."

"There is never an excuse for being a bully." Ruth locked gazes with the surprised conductor. "When I get off this train, I will report your offensive behavior to your superiors."

The conductor's expression changed from belligerent to cautious. "There is no need for that, Ma'am."

Flossie reached across Ruby and laid her hand on Ruth's arm. "Don't make a scene."

Ruth didn't know which she hated more, the conductor's unpardonable behavior or Flossie's meek acceptance of it. She stood and, with one hand, grasped the back of the seat in front of her. At five feet ten inches, she was a head taller than the squat conductor. Her eyes narrowed. "Are you going to apologize to Mrs. Johnson?"

The conductor mumbled a hasty, "Sorry", and moved to the next seats, calling, "Tickets, tickets, please."

Ruth's tone was deadly as a rattler's hiss. "Come back here."

The conductor's head swiveled to stare at her. "Madame--"

Ruth stared him down. "Offer this lady a decent apology."

The conductor removed his cap. "I am very sorry, Mrs. Johnson, if I offended you." He sneered at Ruth. "Is that good enough?"

"It's sufficient." Ruth sat down. The elderly woman in the seat behind her leaned forward. "Good for you, dearie." Tears stood in Flossie's eyes. "Thank you, Mrs. Garland, for coming to my defense, but you shouldn't have. You angered the conductor."

Ruth snorted. "He angered me first, and it's Miss, not Mrs." Her voice softened. "Call me Ruth."

Flossie shifted her sleeping child. "I'd be obliged if you called me Flossie. Are you going to visit someone?"

"I'm going home." *Praise the Lord.*

Flossie fitted her shoulders against her seat. "I'm going home too, in a way. I'm going to stay with Mama and Papa until Mr. Johnson comes home again. He enlisted yesterday after he heard."

"Heard what?" Ruth asked with a frown.

"Heard that the U.S. declared war on Germany. Mr. Johnson predicted sooner or later it would come to pass." She emitted a sigh of reluctant acceptance. "You didn't know? It's in all the papers. Where have you been?"

"I graduated from Baylor Nursing School a few days ago." *I have a diploma and a state certificate as proof.* "Since then, I have been tying up loose ends and packing to go home."

"I didn't know there was a school that taught nursing." Flossie's eyes rounded in surprise. She asked, "What will you do now?"

I wish I knew. Her country was at war. That put a different light on everything. "I had planned to become a medical missionary. Now, I don't know. Maybe before I go anywhere else, I will go to France and help America rid the world of the Kaiser."

A mischievous smile spread across Flossie's face. "For all your good works, you will not be among those who inherit the earth. If the Kaiser met you, he'd run."

It took a moment for her remark to register. Ruth chuckled. "I am not one of the meek among us."

Flossie's smile converted to a frown. "I am, but I wish I wasn't. I wanted to learn to be a telephone operator when I graduated high school. Mr. Johnson wanted us to marry. He said he wouldn't wait. If I wanted to marry him, it was now or never." She sighed. "Sometimes I wonder if he would have waited for me."

"He wouldn't have," Ruth extended her arms. "You must be tired. Let me hold Ruby for a while."

Flossie put Ruby in Ruth's arms. "Thank you." She doubled her fists and stretched her arms over her head. "How do you know?"

Old memories Ruth thought she had lain to rest long ago rose like phantoms in her mind. *Jason, Jason, after all these years, you have the power to inflict pain.* "I had a beau when I was eighteen who told me the same thing. I chose to go to nursing school. He married someone else the next year."

Flossie's voice quivered. "I'm so sorry. Do you still love him?"

Ruth shook her head. "No, and don't be sorry. I am well rid of him."

Chapter Two

Corsicana Train Terminal
Noon, April 7th, 1917

During the layover in Corsicana, as they sat on an ancient bench in the station waiting room, Ruth and Ruby shared the lunch Flossie brought. Ruth was reluctant, at first, to accept Flossie's invitation.

Flossie was adamant. "Please, eat with us. I have enough food here to feed a small army and you have been kind to me. Not many people are -- kind to me, I mean."

Ruth relented. "I will be happy to share your meal."

Lunch consisted of egg and cheese sandwiches and strong green tea flavored with cream, sugar, and lemon. Dessert was round, fat tea cake cookies with a delectable icing.

As they leisurely ate their meal, Flossie told Ruth of her family. She spoke of her parents with love and admiration. "We never had much in the way of worldly goods, but Papa and Mama raised us to know The Lord and to respect them, and love one another. I have four sisters. Two of them are married. Two are still at home. Mama used to wish she had some boys. She says now, she is glad she didn't. They would just march off to war and be killed or come home crippled for life. Do you have any sisters or brothers?"

"I have one sister," Ruth replied. "She's a half-sister, really. We had different fathers."

Flossie poured a second serving of tea from her thermos into Ruth's paper cup. "I like your travel suit, and your shoes. Mr. Johnson doesn't approve of skirts that come only to a woman's mid-calf. He did relent and let me buy a pair of slippers. I didn't ask him about taking off my corset. I just quit wearing it, and hid it in the bottom drawer of my chest."

Ruth's opinion of Mr. Johnson fell to a new low. Time was too short, and her acquaintance with Flossie too new, to offer advice. She smiled. "Shall we go outside and wait for the train?"

The ride from Corsicana to Waco was pleasant, thanks to the company of Flossie and Ruby. The two women exchanged addresses as the train pulled into the Corsicana train station.

The train puffed to a halt. Ruth gathered her things together. "Promise me you will write."

Flossie made an X across her heart. "I promise."

Ruth debarked and stopped before the scowling conductor. "If you so much as hint at trying to intimidate Mrs. Johnson between here and Austin, she will tell me, and I will write letters of complaint to President Wilson, Senator Sheppard, Governor Ferguson, and the president of this railroad line." She stared down at him. "Do you understand?"

The conductor growled. "You are threatening me."

Ruth shot back, "I am promising you."

A large hand wrapped around her upper arm. "The lady means what she says."

Few men were taller than Ruth Garland. This man was. She turned and looked up into the face of Jason Abbott. Four years had taken a toll. The boy she left behind had become a man. She snatched away her arm. "Unhand me."

Jason ignored her request, once more took her arm, and led her toward the waiting room. "Give me your baggage tickets." He ushered her inside.

Once there, Ruth yanked free. Their parting four years ago was not an amiable one. Seeing him now, so mature, calm and collected, fired her anger. "What are you doing here?"

"I came to fetch you home."

"Rachel and Henry are coming for me." Ruth found a seat and sat down.

Jason sat beside her. "They won't be here. Mr. Jarrett hired me to come in their stead."

"Hired you?" Henry Jarrett was as unpredictable as he had always been. "My brother-in-law sent you to fetch me?" Ruth got a grip on her emotions. "Why would he do that?"

Jason put his right thumb to his temple and rubbed his fingers across his brow. "Rachel is not up to the trip. Mr. Jarrett elected to stay with her. He needed a strong man with a wagon and team. I needed the money. Here I am. Give me your baggage stubs. I will load your bags."

Ruth had more than a few bags. Her earthly possessions came with her on that train. They must be in the baggage room by now. She offered Jason the stubs. "What is ailing Rachel?"

"Mr. Jarrett didn't say." Jason took the stubs, and stared down at them. "I'll pull my wagon to the loading dock. This may take a while."

Ruth sat, staring into space, and tried to pull her scattered thoughts together. Seeing Jason so unexpectedly sent her emotions spinning like a toy top. Her mind jumped to another concern. Why was he so reluctant to answer questions about Rachel? She breathed a little easier as a smile spread across her face. Rachel must be pregnant again. Of course, that was it. This would be number four. Maybe it would be another little girl to go with sweet little Pearl Rose. It could be another boy. Heaven forbid it should be another set of twin boys. Joseph and Jacob were enough to keep Rachel busy trying to stay up with them.

Jason tapped her on the shoulder. "Are you ready to go?"

Ruth stood. "Yes." *I am ready, oh so ready to go home.*

Ruth climbed up the wheel of Jason's wagon and sat beside him on the high seat of his buckboard. They drove down Main Street and turned left toward Cedar Gap. The sights and sounds were familiar. This was her home. She grew up here among the cacti, cedars, and underbrush. The blue sky was a welcome sight. The twittering birds were music to her ears. "I love this part of the world."

Jason had not spoken since their journey began. He broke his silence. "I would love it more if it would rain. The drought is playing havoc with my planting."

"Cotton planting time is not until mid-May. You can plant as late as mid-June. Hopefully, we will have rain before then." Ruth turned to stare at the man beside her. He was struggling with a weightier problem than planting cotton. "What is *really* troubling you?"

Jason glanced in her direction. Their eyes met briefly before he looked away. "Clara, my wife, is expecting a baby in late July. It will be the second. We have a two-year-old son."

Why should he be troubled about having another child? "That's great news. Congratulations."

Jason gave his reins a flip. "It is and it isn't. Clara had a difficult time birthing little Leon. She's been sickly through this pregnancy. I worry about her."

Ruth asked, "What does the doctor say?"

"She hasn't seen a doctor," Jason admitted ruefully.

Jason knew better than to put his wife and their baby's health at risk Ruth's temper flared. "Why not?"

Jason's voice fell to a raspy whisper. "I haven't had the money."

Ruth's righteous indignation took command. "Dr. Mullins never demands prompt payment for his services. He is willing to wait until you can pay." She recalled her mother's extended illness. "Mr. Jarrett paid the last of Mama's medical expenses after he and Rachel married. Get your wife to Dr. Mullins immediately."

"She refuses to go. She says we have no right to ask Dr. Mullins to deliver a second child when we have yet to pay him for delivering the first one." The pained expression on Jason's face told of his concern.

"Nonsense," Ruth snapped. "Get--"

"I will work this out," Jason assured her. He paused, and drew a long breath. "I know I have no right to ask this, not after all that happened between us. Would you--?" He paused once more and sighed.

"What happened between us is over and done." Ruth realized, as she spoke, that it had been for a long time.

"You don't hate me?" Jason stared briefly in her direction as his frown converted to a questioning grin.

"No." *Not anymore.* That was true. The last lingering hint of animosity toward the troubled man beside her had wafted away on the wings of passing time. "We should have resolved this matter long ago. What is it you want to ask me?"

"Would you call on Clara? Don't tell her I sent you. Make it a neighborly visit."

They rolled over a big bump in the road, sending them both bouncing around on the buckboard seat. Ruth held on for dear life. "I can't make a medical evaluation from a neighborly call, besides, I'm not an M. D."

"I understand." The tightening of Jason's facial muscles was the only clue to his disappointment.

"No, you don't." A woman and an unborn child needed Ruth's help. The circumstances surrounding that need were unimportant. "What day shall I call?"

Chapter Three

Cedar Gap, Texas
Saturday Evening
April 7th, 1917

Twilight was deepening to night when Jason stopped his wagon in front of the Jarrett's Victorian home. "If you like, I can unload your belongings tomorrow."

Ruth pitched her satchel to the ground, and climbed down from the wagon seat. "Tomorrow is Sunday. I will be in church." She bit her tongue to keep from telling him that was where he should be also. Why mention one of the many things they fought about in the past? "Bring them Monday. I will pay you extra for storage." She straightened her skirt and picked up her satchel.

Jason whistled to his team and called as he pulled away. "We can settle that Monday."

Ruth walked across the gingerbread trimmed porch, and knocked on the front door. In a few minutes she would see Rachel. Her heart sang with joy.

A chubby, middle-aged woman answered her knock. "You must be Miss Ruth. I'm Mrs. Murphy, the housekeeper."

Since when did Rachel have a housekeeper? Ruth assumed it was since she was expecting another baby. She pushed around Mrs. Murphy and stepped into the foyer. "Where is my sister?"

"Mr. Jarrett would like to speak to you in his office before you go in to see Mrs. Jarrett."

"Whatever Mr. Jarrett has to say can wait." Ruth was set to say much more when the intimidating figure of Henry Jarrett loomed in the doorway. He had changed since she last saw him four years ago. He looked older, and more distinguished. His jet-black hair was now feathered with gray. He carried himself with that same air of self-assurance. His voice was deep and authoritative. "I assumed you would balk, still stubborn as a mule."

He and Ruth had locked horns many times in the past. She came to live in this magnificent old mansion when she was thirteen-years-old, just after her mother died. Her pre-teen years had not been pleasant ones. Rachel, who was ten years her senior, was her support and best friend through that troubling, traumatic time.

Moving to Mr. Jarrett's home changed everything. Rachel had a husband she adored, and a position to uphold as the wife of the president and major shareholder of the town's only bank. Henry Jarrett didn't frighten her then, and he didn't frightened her now. "Where is my sister, Mr. Jarrett?"

"For once in your life will you bend a little? Your sister is ill. There are some things we need to discuss before we go in to see her." Mr. Jarrett leaned against the door jamb. "For heaven's sake stop calling me Mr. Jarrett. My name is Henry."

The words *we* and *ill* hung like burrs in Ruth's mind. "What is wrong with Rachel, and what do you mean by *we*? I want to talk to my sister alone."

Henry asked abruptly, "Do you love Rachel?"

That was a stupid question. "You know I do."

Henry straightened to his full height. She had forgotten how tall he was. "So do I. Do you doubt that?"

She didn't, not for a moment. Whatever his shortcomings, Henry Jarrett adored his wife. "No."

"Since that seems to be the only thing we can agree on, shall we begin there?"

Ruth nodded. Her precious sister was ill, maybe gravely so. If compromising with Henry Jarrett was to Rachel's benefit, Ruth would do that, but most reluctantly.

Henry turned and motioned with his hand. "Follow me."

With a sense of foreboding that bordered on panic, Ruth followed him down the hall.

Henry's office was the one room in this sprawling house that was always locked. Ruth had lived here for five years. She had never been inside Henry's private space. She hadn't thought to wonder why then, now she did.

Henry unlocked the door, and stood aside, waiting for her to enter.

Ruth stepped into a spacious, well-furnished room. The furniture was old, but well preserved. The style was Victorian. Shelves of books lined one wall. A huge mahogany desk sat near one of the drape-covered windows. It had a hide leather writing surface and a pith base that undoubtedly covered castors.

Henry sat in a rounded revolving office chair and rolled it behind his desk. "Impressive, isn't it? It was once my father's office. I have kept everything as he left it." He pointed toward a leather wing-backed chair near his desk. "Sit down."

Ruth sat. The leather was buttery-soft. "Say what you have to say. I'm anxious to see Rachel."

The desk Henry sat behind was large and imposing. It would have dwarfed most men. It only added to Henry's commanding presence. Was he trying to impress her or intimidate her? He had not succeeded in doing either. "Are you going to tell me what is so important that it must be said before I see my sister?"

Henry clasped his hands together and laid them on his desk top. "Rachel is terminally ill." His voice broke on what was dangerously near a sob. "She has breast cancer."

Ruth's world crumbled and fell in little pieces around her as the words *terminally ill* ran around inside her head like an evil little hobgoblin. After an agony of silence, she whispered, "How long?"

Henry swallowed and cleared his throat before saying, "Weeks at the most, maybe days, more than likely, hours."

Ruth Garland learned early in life the futility of tears. She had not wept since she was a small child. She sat tall and straight in her chair as a rip of anguish clawed at her heart. "Why didn't you write me? I could have come home and cared for her."

Tears clouded the blue of Henry's eyes. "That was the one thing she didn't want. She knew how important completing nursing school was to you."

By sheer force of will, Ruth withheld the tears that begged to be shed. "Nothing is more important to me than my sister."

Henry took a handkerchief from his pocket and blotted his eyes. "Are you sure?"

How could he ask such a question? "I am more than sure. I am positive. She, Joe, Jake, and Pearl Rose are all I have in this world."

Henry stuffed his handkerchief into his shirt pocket. "That affirmation makes my task easier. Rachel is going to ask much of you. If you don't want to commit, tell me before we go in to see her."

How could he doubt her word? "Whatever Rachel asks of me, I will do."

Henry turned his head to one side and stared at her for several seconds. "You will commit to doing what your sister asks, before she asks it?"

The pain in Ruth's chest tightened. Every minute she wasted arguing with Henry was one less minute she would have to spend with Rachel. "I am going to my sister."

Henry stood and pushed his chair back. "Don't you wish to hear Rachel's requests before we go in to see her?"

Ruth moved toward the door. "Stop wasting time and take me to Rachel."

Henry led her to a bedroom suite on the first floor, rapped on the door, and waited.

A woman's voice questioned from the other side. "Mr. Jarrett?"

Henry answered in the affirmative as he opened the door, and stepped back.

Ruth walked into the dimly lit room. She was met by a tall angular woman wearing a nurse's uniform. The woman extended her hand. "You must be Mrs. Jarrett's sister. She has been asking for you."

Henry followed Ruth into the room. "Ruth, this is Mrs. Dailey. She is Rachel's night nurse."

Ruth shook the woman's hand and acknowledged the introduction as she looked toward the woman who lay on the large bed on the far side of the room. Her blood ran cold. Rachel was thin to the point of emaciation. Her eyes sank far back into her head. A shadow of a smile crossed her face. She lifted a boney hand. "Ruth, little sister, you are here at last--" Lack of breath stopped her words in mid-sentence.

"Big sister, how happy I am to see you."

A flood of sweet memories stirred inside Ruth. It had long been a joke between the two of them. Ruth, who was the younger sister was tall and forceful. Rachel, the older sister was tiny and shy. Tears she swore she would not shed were dangerously near the surface. Ruth came across the room and sat on the side of Rachel's bed. "Henry says you have something to ask me. Ask anything."

"Mr. Jarrett," Mrs. Dailey interrupted to say, "with your permission, I will take a short break. Ring for me before you leave."

Henry nodded his permission as he sat on the other side of Rachel's bed and took her hand in his. "Don't exert yourself, my dear. Rest before you speak again."

Rachel nodded, closed her eyes, and sighed.

Panic lodged in Ruth's throat. Her sister was dying. This was her opportunity to repay Rachel for her love and kindness through the years. "What would you have me do?"

Rachel took a deep breath. "I can't bear the thought of anyone else bringing up my children. *Gasp* Promise me you will do that for me. Bring them up in the church. Teach them to love Jesus. Show them how to live a Christian life."

"I promise." *Was this God's way of saying no to her plans to serve Him as a medical missionary?*

Rachel tightened her hold on Henry's hand. "There is one other thing. Henry agrees. If you give me your word, I can die in peace."

Ruth was hit by a stab of agony that was as painful as it was intense. She could not deny Rachel's last request, no matter what it may be. "I give you my most solemn word."

"When I am gone, will you marry Henry?"

The ceiling of Ruth's reality crashed around her, changing everything in one explosive instant. Surprise trapped her answer in her throat.

"Please," Rachel begged, "please. Give me your word." Tears streamed from her eyes, ran down the sides of her face, and onto her pillow.

There was no time to ponder or consider. Ruth must make a life-altering commitment, or say no to her dying sister's last request, and she must do it now. If she said yes, her life would never be the same again.

Rachel whispered, "Give me your word."

The enormity of what she was promising hit Ruth with the swiftness of a fist punching into her stomach. Dared she make such a commitment? She hesitated for a second. Dared she say no to her dying sister? Her answer rang loud and clear. "I give you my word."

Rachel placed Ruth's hand in Henry's, and laid her skeletal fingers over their hands. "Say it again, both of you."

Ruth stared into Henry's eyes. He looked as hesitant as she felt. She spoke slowly and distinctly. "I give you my word. I will marry Henry."

Henry echoed Ruth's vow. "I give you my word. I will marry Ruth." Tears ran down his cheeks.

Ruth had never before seen a grown man cry. She looked away to stare at the table beside Rachel's bed. The tears she was determined not to shed ran from her eyes and rolled down her cheeks.

Rachel closed her eyes. "Thank you, Jesus. I'm ready now to go home."

Chapter Four

Cedar Gap, Texas
Sunday Morning
April 8th, 1917

The sun climbed into the eastern sky, and shone through Ruth's bedroom window. She opened her eyes. It took a while to recognize her surroundings. This was the room she claimed as her own from the time she came to live with Rachel and Henry, until the day she left for nursing school.

Her reinstatement to her previous quarters came after a pitched battle with Mrs. Murphy. Ruth was preparing for bed, when Mrs. Murphy came, unannounced, through the door. "You are in the wrong room, Miss Garland. Your bedroom is on the third floor."

Ruth laid her brush aside. "I prefer to remain here."

Mrs. Murphy's doughy face set in grim lines. "Mr. Jarrett's bedroom is on this floor. It is only right and proper that, for your visit here, you reside on a separate floor." She picked up Ruth's satchel. "Come along."

The woman's arrogance sparked Ruth's anger. There was no time like the present to set Mrs. Murphy straight on some issues. "My stay here is permanent. This is my bedroom. The subject is closed."

"Really, Miss Garland, it is my duty as Mr. Jarrett's housekeeper to keep order and decorum in his home. I must tell you--"

Ruth cut her short. "As Mr. Jarrett's housekeeper it is your duty to clean and cook." She was weary from lack of sleep and saddened by Rachel's illness. "Furthermore before you assign sleeping quarters in this house to anyone else, you will consult me." That should shut the old biddy up for a while.

It didn't. Mrs. Murphy grabbed the doorknob and glared at Ruth. "I will speak to Mr. Jarrett about this. I should warn you. I am his friend as well as his housekeeper." She dropped Ruth's satchel, strutted through the door, and marched down the hall.

Last night Ruth was too weary to pay heed to Mrs. Murphy's threats. This morning they hopped back into her head like unwelcome callers. Could it be that this middle-aged, overweight woman had designs on Henry? That was a ridiculous thought, or was it? Mrs. Murphy must be in her late forties. Henry was forty-three. Did he...? Had they...? Surely not. That nagging doubt persisted.

She had church services to attend, but not before she saw her niece and nephews, and had breakfast.

Ruth argued with herself before deciding to wear her green and white plaid dress with a tiny collar, ruffled front and mid-calf length slim skirt. She slipped into the dress, shoved her arms into her long matching jacket, and put her feet into her black nurse's oxfords. They made her an inch taller.

She sat before her mirror, and tried to tame her wild mane of hair by pulling it into a knot at the nape of her neck. By the time she secured the knot, hair strands had escaped to frame her face with pixie curls. Fine for dainty damsels. Not at all fitting for an almost six foot tall, one hundred-fifty pound woman.

Ruth snorted her disgust, tossed her brush on her dresser and slammed out the door. She stood, grasping the knob and catching her breath before hurrying down the hall to what had once been Pearl Rose's bedroom. She had not seen her niece in four years. Would Pearl Rose have even a slight recollection of her? She rapped on the door.

A childish voice called from inside, "Go away."

Surprise put a catch in Ruth's voice. "It's your Aunt Ruth, Pearl Rose. Please let me come in." She waited several seconds. There was no answer. Ruth knocked again. "Pearl Rose?"

The door opened slowly. Pearl Rose peeked from behind it. "I thought you were Mrs. Murphy." She opened the door a little wider. "Are you *really* my aunt?

"I am indeed. May I come in?"

Pearl Rose stepped from behind the door and swung it open. "Mama said you were coming."

The child wore a white muslin dress with an embroidered yoke and puffed sleeves, white lisle stockings and Mary Jane style shoes. Her dark hair hung down her back in long, soft curls. Her resemblance to Rachel was uncanny. Pain, begotten by regret, held Ruth in its grip. Rachel would never watch her daughter grow up, walk down the aisle, marry, have children. *Why, God, why?* "I arrived last evening. You have grown since I last saw you." She had to know. "Do you remember me?"

"A little. Mama talks about you a lot. Sometimes she tells us stories about when you were a little girl. She says you are very brave and I should grow up to be like you."

Last night, in the solitude of her room, Ruth couldn't stop her tears. Now, new ones found their way into her throat. She batted her eyes and swallowed. How much did Pearl Rose know about Rachel's illness? "We must both be brave. We have difficult days ahead."

Pearl Rose flung her small arms around Ruth's waist. "Is my mama *really* going to die?"

Ruth sat in a chair, lifted the child into her lap, and held her close. "Your mama is going to heaven to live with Jesus."

Pearl Rose lifted her tear stained face and stared up at Ruth. "Does she have to die to go there?"

How inadequate Ruth felt. "Your mother is suffering now. She will be free from pain when she goes to be with Jesus."

"You sound like Papa, never giving me a straight answer."

The pain in Ruth's chest tightened. "Yes, your mama is going to die. I will be here for you when she is gone. I will never leave you." She was making long-term, life-altering commitments to a dying woman and an eight-year-old child. *Dear God, help me to always to keep them.*

Pearl Rose slid from Ruth's lap. "Papa is going to be sad too. Will you be here for him when Mama goes to live with Jesus?" She leaned her elbows on Ruth's lap and looked up into her face, waiting for an answer.

A quiver traveled down Ruth's spine. *Being there* for Henry took on a broader meaning. "Yes. I will."

Pearl Rose asked on a breathless sigh, "Will you kiss my cheek the way Mama did when she came for me in the mornings?"

Ruth leaned down and kissed the velvety softness of Pearl Rose's cheek. *This child is starved for a mother's love.* Self-doubt, an alien emotion to Ruth Garland, crept into the hollow of her heart. *What if I can't do this?* She thought of her sister lying at death's door. *I can, because I must. God, show me the way.*

Ruth stood. "Would you like me to tie a ribbon in your hair before we go downstairs?" The dress Pearl Rose wore went out of style in 1910. The long stockings should be replaced with ankle length socks.

Pearl Rose clapped her hands. "Oh, yes. Yes. I would love to wear a ribbon in my hair every day."

"Why don't you?" Ruth asked.

"Mrs. Murphy says ribbons are for Sundays and special occasions."

Anger erupted inside Ruth. "Mrs. Murphy is no longer in charge here. Bring me a ribbon."

Pearl Rose bounced across the room and rummaged in her dresser drawer. "May I wear a red ribbon even though it's Sunday?"

"You may wear any color you choose."

Ruth wrapped the ribbon around Pearl Rose's curls, tied it at the nape of her neck, and pulled it into a huge bow before standing back to admire her handiwork. "You look beautiful."

The child's big brown eyes, so like her mother's, glowed with pleasure. "Thank you, Aunt Ruth."

Ruth took her hand. "Let's go downstairs and I'll make breakfast. Shall we stop on the way for Jacob and Joseph?"

"Oh, yes." Pearl Rose said before she asked, "Will you cook oatmeal?"

Ruth opened the door and turned down the hall. "Do you like oatmeal?"

"Not very well." Pearl Rose stopped before a door near the stairway. "This is Joe and Jake's room." She rapped on the door.

A little boy's voice called from the other side, "Go away. Leave us alone."

"That's Jake," Pearl Rose explained. She rapped again. "It's me, Rosie."

A gruffer voice responded. "I'm coming."

"That's Joe." Pearl Rose stood, patiently waiting.

The door opened. A husky, freckled-faced boy stood on the other side smiling at them. He wore knickers, oxfords, knee-high socks, and a spotless white shirt. "Good morning, Rosie, and Ma'am."

Pearl Rose giggled. "She's not a ma'am. She's our Aunt Ruth. Remember how Mama said she would soon be here?"

Joe extended his hand. "I am pleased to meet you, Aunt Ruth." He grinned at his sister. "I like your red ribbon, but I don't think Mrs. Murphy will approve."

"Aunt Ruth says we don't have to mind Mrs. Murphy anymore."

That wasn't *exactly* what Ruth said, but it was near enough.

The skinny child who came to stand behind Joe had the physical appearance of a street urchin. His hair was tousled, his stockings sagged, and his shirt was buttoned incorrectly. The scowl on his elfin face was not a harbinger of good tidings. She extended her hand. "Good morning, Jacob. I am your Aunt Ruth."

"My name is Jake." He ignored her hand.

Ruth dropped her arm, and walked toward the stairway. "Shall we go downstairs and have breakfast?"

Pearl Rose fell in step with her.

Joe and Jake followed along behind. Jake said, "Pearl Rose is not my sister's name either. It's Rosie."

Ruth looked down at the little girl who clung to her hand.

Pearl Rose smiled up at her. "You can call me Rosie, if you'd like. It's my special name that Mama, Papa, Joe, and Jake call me."

A warm feeling filled Ruth's chest and ran through her body. "Thank you, Rosie."

Rosie looked over her shoulder. "We won't be having oatmeal this morning. Aunt Ruth is making breakfast, and she doesn't like oatmeal either."

The scowl on Jake's face disappeared to be replaced by a mischievous smile. "Old Mrs. Murphy makes oatmeal every Sunday morning."

Ruth descended the stairs. "You should be more respectful of Mrs. Murphy." She wondered with each descending step she took, how she should go about handling a potentially volatile situation.

Chapter Five

The kitchen was warm and sunny. A large wood cook stove with chrome and porcelain-finished doors, covered much of one wall. A warming cabinet supported by a porcelain back stood above six cast-iron burners. Ruth touched the stovetop. "Cold as January." She opened the water reservoir on the stove's right side. "Empty."

The three children climbed into chairs about the round table that stood in the middle of the floor, and exchanged knowing glances.

Ruth opened the wood box. "Not even chips."

Joe scooted from his chair and stood. "Sometimes Jake and me get the wood for Mrs. Murphy. Do you want us to bring in some logs for you?"

Ruth kept her voice calm. Inside she seethed with anger. It was not Mrs. Murphy's place to assign tasks to her niece and nephews. "You can help me."

Rosie hopped to her feet. "Do you want me to make the coffee? I know how." She pointed to the coffee pot on the back of the stove. "Mrs. Murphy gets it ready the night before. All I have to do is put it on a back burner of the stove. You will have to move it when it percolates. Mrs. Murphy says I shouldn't move things around on a hot stove. I might get burned."

"Please do." Maybe Mrs. Murphy had more sense that Ruth gave her credit for having. "Mrs. Murphy is right, you shouldn't get near a hot stove." She motioned for the boys to come with her. It took some time, but the three of them brought in several logs, and Ruth made a fire.

The children sat, once again, around the table.

Ruth put on the apron that hung on a hook near the cupboard. "What do you want for breakfast?"

Of one accord, they shouted, "Pancakes."

Pancakes she could do. She found a griddle and put it on the stove, and looked in the Hoosier *(A large metal container used to keep rats, mice and other vermin from contaminating foodstuff stored there*). She located a box of pancake mix. "Hey, kids, set the table."

They set about to do her bidding, laughing and talking as they collected, plates, knives, forks, and glasses.

The ice box was across the room from the stove. It too, was porcelain and big, with three doors and brass hardware with hinged door closures. Ruth found a quart bottle of milk, and rummaged around inside the box looking for butter.

Rosie put plates around the table. "Mrs. Murphy says not to shop in the ice box, especially on Sunday. The iceman doesn't come today."

Jake came to stand behind her. He pointed to a far corner of the box. "The butter is back there."

Ruth retrieved it, and gave it to him. "Put this on the table."

Jake put the butter on the table and moved toward the pantry. "I'll get the syrup and the honey too."

By the time Ruth mixed pancake batter, the griddle was piping hot. She dropped three big blobs of batter on it, and watched until they bubbled on top, before she flipped them over.

Breakfast was a huge success. Rosie and Jake laughed and talked as they ate. Joe was more reserved, but he smiled at the antics of Rosie and Jake.

From somewhere in the back of the house, Mrs. Murphy appeared to stand in a doorway. "What is going on here?"

Rosie and Jake fell silent. Joe's smile vanished.

Don't lose your temper in the presence of the children. "We are having breakfast." By sheer force of will Ruth held onto her patience.

Mrs. Murphy put her hands on her ample hips. Ignoring Ruth, she spoke to the children. "You know you are not to leave your rooms in the mornings until I come to fetch you." She pointed toward the stairway. "Get back up those stairs and stay in your rooms until I come for you."

Ruth's anger exploded like an erupting volcano. She turned in her chair until she could stare into Mrs. Murphy's doughy face. "Rosie, Jake, Joe, stay where you are." Without taking her eyes off the woman who still stood in the doorway, she said, "I thought you and I had come to an understanding." She stood, and advanced toward the housekeeper. "Obviously, we have not."

Footsteps sounding nearer and nearer stopped her tirade. Henry came from the dining room. "Come quickly, Ruth. Children, you too. Mama is asking to see you." Ruth followed behind the children. Before stepping into the hallway, she paused. "If you want to keep your job, clean this kitchen before I return."

She sped away, hurrying to catch up to Henry. He was almost to Rachel's bedroom door before she reached him. "Slow down."

Henry stopped and turned to face her. Grief carved itself into every line of his face. His pain-laden whisper spoke volumes. "Rachel is dying--"

Ruth opened her mouth to speak.

Henry's warning stare stopped her. "Wait here." He shepherded Rosie and the twins into Rachel's bedroom, followed them, and closed the door.

Ruth dropped her head and clenched her teeth as a wave of pain rocked through her. Rachel was dying -- not sometime soon, or tomorrow, but now, this instant. She bowed her head as her aching heart hardened. *Why, God, why?* What terrible thing had she done that He would take Rachel from her?

She looked up when Henry and the children came from Rachel's room. Joe and Rosie were crying. Jake sniffled and wiped his nose on his shirt sleeve.

Dr. Mullins followed.

A grim faced Henry passed her without speaking or looking her way, and guided his children down the hall toward the stairs.

Dr. Mullins came to stand beside Ruth. "Brace yourself, my dear. You must be brave."

Ruth wanted to scream and rage against the injustice of death claiming her precious Rachel. "Why, Dr. Mullins, why, why?"

"God's ways are past our knowing." Dr. Mullins put his arm around her shoulders, and led her into Rachel's room.

The smell of death permeated the chamber and wrapped around Ruth like a shroud. The journey to Rachel's bed was a thousand miles. Ruth began it on trembling legs.

Rachel extended her arms. "Ruth, little sister, come and sit beside me."

Ruth's vision narrowed. All she saw was the face of her dying sister. "Big sister--" Her voice broke.

Rachel smiled. Her gaunt face took on a heavenly radiance. "Don't be sad, or afraid. I'm not."

Ruth knelt at her sister's bedside. "Rachel, I will miss you. I--"

Rachel shushed her. "I have so little time to say so many things. Don't talk, listen."

Ruth held Rachel's cold, gaunt hand in her warm, firm one, and kept silent.

"Take care of my dear children, Ruth. Help my sons grow up to be fine, God-fearing men."

Ruth wanted to say so many things. The words couldn't get past the knot in her throat.

Rachel's breath rattled in her throat, as she gasped. "Watch over Henry. He is a good man, but in some ways he is such a child. Watch his diet. Don't let him smoke too many cigars. His limit is three a day." She closed her eyes, and opened them slowly. "Most of all, watch over my little Rosie, my Rose of Sharon. My Pearl of great price. Don't let her grow up to be weak like me. Teach her to be strong, like you. Promise..." Her voice trailed away on a rattling breath. Her hand fell lifeless to her side.

Grief held Ruth in its grasp. She could neither move nor speak. One irrefutable fact played through her brain like a dirge of doom. Her sweet sister was gone from this earth forever.

Dr. Mullins was by Ruth's side, feeling for a pulse in Rachel's neck. "Your sister is gone." He moved his hand to close Rachel's eyes.

Ruth buried her face in her hands, and wept, great wrenching sobs that shook her body, and crushed her spirit. An anguished cry tore from her throat. "Why, God, why?"

Dr. Mullins put his hands under Ruth's armpits and pulled her to her feet. "You must be strong, my dear. That is what Rachel expects of you."

Ruth was overwhelmed by grief. "Why did God do this to me, and to Rachel, and her family? Why, why?"

Dr. Mullins put his arms around Ruth's shoulders. "Over the next few months, Henry and the children will need some of that strength Rachel was so sure you possess."

A terrible desolation filled Ruth's heart and lodged in the pit of her stomach. She dried her tears. Even though she was the younger, Rachel had always leaned on her for support, encouragement, and yes, strength. Ruth had never let her down, nor did she intend to now. "Has Henry made arrangements for Rachel's funeral and interment?"

"He has not." Dr. Mullins covered Rachel's body with her sheet. "Henry has been in denial for months."

He was in no condition now to make decisions. The sooner Ruth got Rachel's body out of this house, the better it would be for both Henry and the children. "Can you make arrangements to have Rachel's body taken to Rawlins' Funeral Parlor as soon as possible? I will be in tomorrow morning to make arrangements."

"I will have it out within the hour." Dr. Mullins reached for his hat and bag. "Bless you, Ruth."

As the door slammed behind him, Ruth fell to her knees and clasped her hands under her chin. Her God was mighty and strong, stronger than she could ever hope to be. *Forgive me, Father, for questioning the reason for Rachel's death. Help me to accept and not question why. Your ways are past finding out. It is enough to know you love me with a love beyond measure.* With renewed strength, she stood. She must find Henry and the children. They needed her now, and she needed them.

Chapter Six

Cedar Gap, Texas
Monday Evening
October 9th, 1917

The last six months had been the hardest of Ruth's life. She struggled each day to maintain her emotional balance. She had promised Rachel to care for Henry and the children. What an impossible task it was turning out to be. Rosie spent much of each day in her room. She was withdrawn and sullen. Jake became belligerent, constantly teasing Rosie and provoking Joe. That teasing often resulted in screaming matches with Rosie, the provocations brought about fist-fights with Joe, who treated his family as if they were strangers.

Ruth planted a garden, hoping the children would show interest in watching the miracle of growing things. No such luck. Ruth tended it faithfully. She raised a bumper crop, and canned, dried, or stored the surplus in the root cellar. Mrs. Murphy constantly complained about the extra work. So many times, Ruth considered firing this contentious old woman. Knowing she could never manage the house and the children alone stopped her.

Always, Ruth found time to visit Jason and Clara Abbott.

In July, just after Clara delivered a second son, Jason lost his farm and moved his family to Cedar Gap. He found work at the Cedar Gap Feed store.

Ruth continued to visit Clara often.

Occasionally she dropped by the feed store to make a purchase and chat with Jason. She knew he struggled to make ends meet. Once she offered to loan him money. He refused what she intended as a gesture of friendship. "Most certainly not."

She had offended him, and that was not her intent. To apologize would add insult to injury. She changed the subject. "Are you apt to be drafted?"

"I'm in category two," he answered between clenched teeth.

Ruth took that as a no, and left the feed store knowing she had injured an old friend.

She poured out her heart in letters to Flossie. Return mail brought messages filled with sympathy and recordings of Flossie's woes and problems. Mr. Johnson was fighting in France. She prayed each night he wouldn't be "kilt." One of her unmarried sisters was expecting a child. Her parents wanted to toss her out. Flossie intervened and prevailed. "I remembered how you stood up for me and I did the same for my sister. I learnt a lot from you."

Despite the difference in their education and outlook, a bond formed between these two women that would grow and endure for a lifetime.

Late in August a skirmish occurred along the Arizona-Mexican border between American soldiers, and the Mexican military, who was assisted by German military advisors. Germany and their Mexican cohorts could invade the U.S. by crossing the Rio Grande. Uncertain danger loomed too close for comfort. Ruth dug to the bottom of her trunk and found her papa's pistol. She loaded it, and slept with in the locked drawer of her night stand.

Nothing more came of the border skirmish. In September school started and Ruth pushed the event to the back of her mind. More imminent and distressing matters demanded her attention. Each morning was a battle to get each child dressed, fed, and out the door. Each night the fight began all over again, over homework.

Always on the periphery of Ruth's thoughts was her promise to marry Henry. More and more she doubted the wisdom of such a union. Each evening he came home from the bank, went to his office, and stayed there with the door closed. He came out when Ruth called him for dinner. When the meal was over, he retreated again behind his closed office door.

Occasionally Ruth thought about what it would be like to be Henry's wife. She respected him. Despite their former differences, she grew to like him. He was intelligent and thoughtful. He was also in love with her dead sister, and she suspected he always would be. He never mentioned the promise they made to Rachel. Maybe he didn't intend to keep that promise. Maybe it would be just as well if he didn't.

Ruth grabbed her sweater and went to sit in one of the rocking chairs on the veranda. The evening was cool. Autumn in all its rough beauty had returned to Central Texas. Leaves fell from deciduous oak trees and elms. In contrast, evergreen oaks and cedars stood proud and green. Soon cold winds would sweep down from the north. She closed her eyes and let her mind drift.

"Aunt Ruth?"

Ruth opened her eyes to see Rosie standing beside her. *What is it this time? A verbal fight with Jake? Refusal to do her homework?* "Yes, Rosie."

"Will you help me with my homework?"

What brought about this change? Ruth didn't know, but she welcomed it. "I'll be glad to. What can I do?"

"Will you listen to me recite my multiplication tables?"

Twilight, like an obscure thief, crept across the flat countryside. Rosie dragged another chair near Ruth's. "I'll start with my two's and go through my twelve's. Stop me when I make a mistake."

Ruth wasn't sure she remembered her multiplication tables. "Let's go inside so I can see your study sheet. I would hate to make a mistake."

Rosie pointed toward the heavens. Bright stars punched through the darkening sky. "The stars are coming out. Mama says if you wish on a star, your wish might come true."

Sadness tightened in Ruth's chest. "You miss your mama, don't you?"

Tears filled Rosie's eyes. "Aunt Ruth, have I been a bad girl?"

Ruth was appalled that her niece would ask such a question. "Why ever would you think that?"

"Mama said she would watch over Joe and Jake, and me. I pray every night and ask her to answer me when I talk to her. She won't. At first I was mad. Now I'm sad. I have been mean. Is that why Mama won't come back and talk to me?"

How judgmental and unfeeling Ruth had been. "No. Never. Your mama is watching over you. She's watching over all of us."

"Why doesn't she tell us?"

Please, God, give me the words to say. "Heaven is a beautiful place where sickness or death will never come. Jesus has prepared a special home for your mama. She is well and happy there. She doesn't want to come back to earth and be in terrible pain again."

Doubt clouded Rosie's upturned face. "Are you sure?"

In my father's house are many mansions: if it were not so, I would have told you, I go to prepare a place for you. (John 14:2 JKV) The comfort of that promise flooded Ruth's soul. "I am very sure."

Rosie got from her chair and climbed into Ruth's lap. She put her arms round her aunt's neck. "I was afraid Mama didn't love me anymore."

Ruth hugged the child to her. "Your mama loves you very much, and so do I."

With peace came the knowledge that she had failed her sister in the worst possible way. She was neglecting to ground her children in God's word. *Forgive me, Father. From this day forward, there will be Bible reading and prayer in this house each and every day. The children and I will attend church services regularly.*

As would Henry if she could convince him to do so.

Chapter Seven

Cedar Gap, Texas
Saturday Evening
November 25th, 1917

November's blustery days replaced October's bright blue Indian summer. The last two months brought gradual changes in the children's behavior. They now looked forward to Sunday school and church. An established homework hour before dinner, with Ruth in attendance, was a time to ask questions, and discuss events of the day. By early November the household settled into some semblance of order.

Henry remained aloof and distant from Ruth and his children, choosing instead, to spend his evenings in his office. Ruth repeatedly invited him to attend church with her and the children. He always politely refused.

Ruth reasoned, when Rachel diedthat he needed time to grieve for his beloved wife. She hadn't anticipated he would become a hermit. Now she was beginning to wonder.

She was pleased when one Sunday morning after services, Reverend Cooper asked if he and Mrs. Cooper might come to call the next Saturday evening.

Thanksgiving was just around the corner. Maybe the Reverend would ask for a donation to help see that needy families in and around Cedar Gap had food for Thanksgiving. "We would be delighted to have you call." She hoped he would also encourage Henry to attend Church services with her and the children.

Saturday morning Mrs. Murphy grudgingly baked cookies for the occasion.

It would be best if the children were otherwise occupied during the Coopers' visit. Ruth wanted Reverend Cooper to feel free to speak with Henry about spiritual matters.

Saturday afternoon she went shopping. She bought a set of building blocks for each of the boys, and a porcelain doll for Rosie. After dinner she waited for Henry to go to his office. The wait was brief. She took the children to the back parlor where she gave them their unexpected gifts. Rosie and Jake were ecstatic. Even Joe showed surprise. He poured the blocks from their container and onto the floor. "What are these for?"

The gifts were bribes. Ruth was ashamed to admit that, even to herself. "Because you have been such good children I decided to surprise each of you with a gift. The only requirement is you must play with them here, in the back parlor, and nowhere else."

Rosie hugged her doll to her chest. "Not even in our rooms?"

Ruth echoed, "Not even in your rooms." She would change her decree after The Reverend and Mrs. Cooper were gone.

Jake had yet to open his gift. "Does this count against Christmas? Will we get presents then too?"

Ruth's fixed expression converted to a smile. "Santa will still come to see you at Christmas time."

Rosie sat in a chair, rocking the doll in her arms. "Papa told us a long time ago that Santa isn't real."

Jake spilled his blocks onto the floor. "He's a myth, whatever that is."

Ruth's astonishment was swallowed up in anger. The magic of believing in Santa Claus was every child's right. "I will come for you when it is bedtime."

The children were too engaged with their new toys to note her quick exit.

Ruth hurried toward Henry's office. She had yet to tell him The Reverend and Mrs. Cooper would soon call.

The clock in the hall chimed seven. The doorbell rang. She veered to the left, and toward the door. No time now to tell Henry they were expecting callers. He would know soon enough.

Ruth opened the door and extended her arm. "Reverend and Mrs. Cooper, won't you come in?"

Ruth was Rosie's age when she first made the acquaintance of Gladys and Alonzo Cooper, He was the handsome new seminary graduate and the new pastor of the Cedar Gap Baptist Church. He had a wealth of blond hair and a winning personality. Gladys was a slim young girl with a cheery disposition and dimples when she smiled.

Time had changed the three of them. The present Reverend Cooper was a portly, balding man with a bulbous nose and a gentle manner. Today's Mrs. Cooper wore her dark, gray-streaked hair in a bun. The years had not been kind to her. Her dimples were lost in the age lines around her mouth and eyes. Her once slim figure was reduced to a scarecrow skinniness. She wore an expression of perpetual forbearance.

I am the one who has changed the most. Then I was a robust little girl with blonde pigtails and freckles. Today I am a sandy-haired, too tall, full-bodied woman, only my freckles remain. Ruth recognized long ago that she would never be the dainty, beautiful woman her sister grew up to be. For the most part she accepted her weight, her height, her plain features, even her freckles. Now and then, she had to ask, "Why, Dear Lord?"

The moment passed. Ruth ushered The Reverend and his wife into the front parlor. "Please sit down. Mr. Jarrett is in his office. I will--" She turned and skidded to a stop in time to keep from colliding with Henry.

He stepped around Ruth and shook hands with The Reverend and

Gladys. "How nice of you to call. Please sit down." His suave manner should have put his guests at ease. It didn't. Alonzo levered his hefty body into an easy chair. Gladys perched on the seat of a needlepoint covered chair.

Henry sat on the sofa across from The Reverend.

There followed a spate of pin-drop silence.

Ruth stood behind Henry, becoming more uneasy by the minute. "Mrs. Murphy baked cookies this morning. I have fresh coffee. It will only take a minute--" She backed from the room and sped down the hall toward the kitchen.

Once there, she quickly assembled cookies, cups, napkins, and a pot of coffee. She set them on a tray.

"Are you finding everything?"

Ruth turned to see Mrs. Murphy standing in a far corner, almost hidden by shadows. "Where did you come from?" She would have sworn the kitchen was empty.

"I work here, remember?"

It was not her words, but her tone that set Ruth's teeth on edge. "Reverend and Mrs. Cooper came to call." She picked up her tray and left the room. *One of these days that woman is going to push me too far.*

Drinking coffee and enjoying Mrs. Murphy's cookies lessened the tension in the room. By the time Alonzo drank his third cup of coffee and ate the last cookie on the platter, the foursome were relaxed and enjoying polite conversation.

Gladys set her still-full cup on the tray alongside her half-eaten cookie, and caught her husband's eye. "Alonzo, my dear, it's getting late."

Alonzo dusted crumbs from his vest. "Time does get away from one." He cleared his throat. "Mr. Jarrett -- Henry, may I have a word with you in private?"

Confusion slid across Henry's face and was trapped in the blue of his eyes. "I -- Yes, of course." He stood. "Come with me to my office."

Ruth wanted to ask what this was about. Discretion stayed her tongue. She smiled at Gladys "Are you looking forward to Thanksgiving?"

Gladys shrugged her indifference. 'Thanksgiving is too much work with too few rewards."

Ruth knew no answer for that cryptic statement. "Are you expecting guests?"

"Our son and his wife and two daughters are coming from Round Rock."

Carrying on a conversation with this woman was like pulling teeth. "Do they live there now?" *Idiot, why else would they be coming from there?*

"Abraham pastors a church there. It has a membership of over five hundred people."

Was Abraham her son? Ruth couldn't recall. She was not going to make a fool of herself all over again by asking. "How nice." She sat, determined to let Gladys instigate any further conversation.

In a matter of minutes, or was it hours, Alonzo and Henry returned. One look at Henry's stern expression and Ruth knew all was not well.

The Reverend's bleak countenance reinforced her fear. He said a hasty good-bye before adding, "Henry, my friend, I hope you will take into consideration the things we discussed."

Gladys followed her husband out the door without so much as a nod of her head.

The moment the door slammed, Henry exploded. "Mischief is afoot." He grabbed Ruth's hand and dragged her toward his office. "I intend to get to the bottom of this."

The bottom of what? "The children are in the back parlor. Let me put them to bed--"

Henry didn't break his stride. "This won't wait."

Chapter Eight

Cedar Gap, Texas
Saturday Night
November 24th, 1917

Ruth pulled free of Henry's grasp. "Whatever you have to say can wait another thirty minutes." She walked, with her head held high, down the hall toward the back parlor.

Henry called after her, "If it takes three hours, come to my office when the task is done. I can't sleep with this on my mind."

Ruth raised her arm and waved her hand as she slipped into the back parlor.

Joe was asleep on the floor. Jake had claimed Joe's blocks, as well as his own to erect a tall, shaky fortification. "Look Aunt Ruth, the Tower of Babel."

Rosie cuddled in a chair with her doll. "Be quiet, you will wake Joe and my baby."

Jake's answer was to strike the building with a swift swipe of one hand. Blocks flew in all directions. One struck Joe's leg.

Joe sat up and rubbed his eyes. "What happened?" He looked around and wailed, "Jake stole my blocks."

Ruth was weary and upset. She wanted to crawl into bed and sleep for hours. That wasn't apt to happen until she dealt with what Henry had on his mind. "Tomorrow morning Jake will return your blocks." She sent Jake a look that dared him to argue. "Rosie, you may take your dolly with you. Let's go."

"'What about Joe and me?" Jake whined. "Can we take our blocks?"

"Not until tomorrow after you put Joe's blocks in their box and return them to him with an apology."

"That's not fair," Joe howled. "Why should I be in trouble because Jake has been bad?"

Ruth took Joe's hand. "I will make it up to you." She was doing this all wrong. She shouldn't bribe these children. At this moment she was willing to take the path of least resistance. "You can go shopping with me the next time I go." She herded the trio into the hall.

Rosie stopped. "May I go too?"

"Yes, move along."

Jake let out a blood-curdling scream. "That's not fair. I wanna go too."

Henry stuck his head out his office door. "Merciful heavens, what is going on out here?"

Jake bellowed, "I want to go too."

Henry directed his question to Ruth. "Go where?"

Since Rachel passed away, Henry had paid no attention to his children. Why would he choose now, of all times, to be a concerned parent? "Go back into you lair. I can handle this."

"It doesn't appear so." Henry crouched down to be on eye level with Jake. "What's wrong, little fellow?"

Ruth threw up her hands in disgust. "You're right. They are your children. *You* put them to bed."

"It's not fair, Papa," Jake complained.

"Jake stole my blocks," Joe shouted.

Rosie held her doll out for Henry to see. "Look, Papa. Aunt Ruth bought me a present."

A cacophony of voices arose as each child vied for Henry's attention. *How starved they are for their papa's love.*

Henry stood and stepped into the hall. "Calm down and speak one at a time. We can settle this amiably. Ruth?"

Ruth stood in the doorway of Henry's office. "Come to your office when the task is done. I can't sleep until I know what's on your mind. I will be waiting. Good luck." She shut the door.

Footsteps and voices sounded down the hall, grew faint, and faded away.

Ruth collapsed in the leather chair. What must she be thinking to behave so rudely? *He had it coming.* She rested her head on the softness of the chair back. *I can't do this.* She closed her eyes. *Dear God, why?* Her eyelids grew heavy...

A large hand shook her to wakefulness. "Ruth?"

Ruth opened her eyes to see Henry standing over her. "Are the children asleep?"

'"Don't you know?" Henry eased his bulk down onto the couch.

Ruth sat up and shook off sleep's embrace. "Know what?"

"If the children are asleep. You said you couldn't sleep until you knew what was on my mind. You were asleep. Are you clairvoyant?"

He was deliberately trying to provoke her. She should have expected as much. Her mind hearkened back to earlier times when he used his sarcasm to make her feel childish and inadequate. "I am no longer a teenager, old man."

Henry's face set in hard lines. "Old man, am I?" He stopped as his shoulders slumped. "I did not realize until tonight what a great responsibility Rosie, Joe, and Jake are. I will be more attentive to them in the future. You have my permission to hire a nursemaid to help you, if you'd like."

His sudden about-face surprised Ruth. "I would like. Thank you."

"That's settled." Henry leaned back and crossed one ankle over the other. "Now onto the reason for Reverend Cooper's visit."

This has to be bad news. Ruth braced herself. "Yes?"

"There is talk around town about you and me living under the same roof. Reverend Cooper came to warn me. He was most reluctant to do so, but he felt it his duty."

"Talk?" Ruth snorted. "It is not 'talk', it is gossip. I should have been privy to that conversation. I could have set him straight in a scant second. Who started this vicious lie? I--"

Henry held up his hands to stop her rant. "Don't kill the messenger. Reverend Cooper has our best interest at heart."

Ruth pressed her palms to her cheeks. "I could rent a room at Mrs. Yancy's boarding house."

"The children are attached to you. To have you go so soon after losing their mother, would be devastating. If you are willing to hold to your pledge to Rachel, so am I. We can be married."

Ruth gripped the arms of her chair. In a matter of moments, a dozen dissenting questions raced through her mind. The answer to each one was the same. *You promised, you promised, you promised.* As a teenager, she never knew where she stood with this man, and she didn't know now. "I would never break a promise I made to Rachel."

A frown creased Henry's brow. "Then it's settled?"

It wasn't, not by a long shot. "When you say marriage, how much--" She paused. "How far--?" For the first time in a long time, Ruth Garland was at a loss for words.

Henry's frown converted to a grin. "How much do you expect from an old man? How far do you think I *could* go?"

He was doing it again, making her feel like a not-too-bright child. "You know what I mean." Heat burned in her cheeks.

"Are you asking me if I expect you to attend to *all* your wifely duties?"

She was, she may as well admit it. "Do you?"

Henry stood and walked toward the door. "That, my dear, is your decision, not mine. Good night." He opened the door and waited for her to go.

Ruth paused at the entrance. "You arrange for the ceremony." She stepped into the hall. "Find a Baptist minister to perform the nuptials. I refuse to stand before a judge or justice-of-the-peace and recite holy vows."

Ruth climbed the stairs. A knot of pain wedged in her stomach. They were making a mockery of those holy vows. The wedding was bogus, the marriage a sham. Why should she care who read meaningless pledges? For the first time since she was a small child, Ruth cried herself to sleep.

She awoke the next morning refreshed from a good night's rest and steadfast in her decision to make the best of a bad situation. This was Sunday. She was determined to continue attending church services. If anyone there dared say one word about her living "under the same roof" with Henry, they would wish they hadn't.

Much to Ruth's surprise, Sunday services moved along smoothly. By the time Reverend Cooper said his last amen, she decided she had worried needlessly. She left as quickly as possible. No need to tempt fate.

Chapter Nine

Cedar Gap, Texas
Monday Morning
November 26th, 1917

Monday morning Ruth woke to a bright and sunny late November day. She dressed, collected the children, and ushered them downstairs, to find Henry sitting at the kitchen table nursing a cup of coffee. He was usually gone before they came down.

Mrs. Murphy served the children scrambled eggs, bacon, and biscuits. After their first altercation over oatmeal for breakfast, Ruth threatened her with dismissal if she ever served it again. She wiped her hands on her apron and asked in a civilized tone, if Ruth would like a cup of coffee.

She's on her best behavior because Henry is present. Maybe Ruth should demand he appear for breakfast every morning. "Yes, thank you." She turned her attention to Henry. Why was he here? She wanted to ask. She didn't dare, not with Mrs. Murphy hanging onto every word he spoke. "Good morning, Henry."

Henry's nod acknowledged her greeting. "I thought I would go with you as you walk the children to school this morning."

His announcement elicited a "Hooray" from Rosie, a "whoopee" from Jake, and a delighted smile from Joe.

Mrs. Murphy dropped a pan. It fell to the floor. The sound of the crash echoed around the room. She picked it up and put it on the stove. "Excuse me." She walked from the room and toward the back of the house.

"She's angry," Jake said.

Henry pushed his coffee cup from him. "She's not angry, son, she's embarrassed. Shall we be on our way?"

Ruth squelched the thought there might be some ulterior reason for Henry's out-of-the-blue decision to accompany her and the children to school. He had recently said he would be more attentive to his children in the future. "We will be pleased to have you walk with us."

The walk to school was pleasant. Rosie clung to Henry's hand. "It's a lovely day, isn't it, Papa?"

Henry smiled down at her. "Indeed it is."

Jake skipped ahead, announcing to everyone he met, "My papa is walking to school with me."

Joe was content to hang onto Henry's other hand.

They reached the school. The children said their reluctant good-byes and went inside to classes.

Ruth said good-bye to Henry and turned to begin her journey toward Jason and Clara's home.

Henry caught up to her. "This is not the way home. Where are you going?"

Ruth explained somewhat reluctantly, "This is the day I visit Clara Abbott and her little boys."

Henry scowled. "Are you still going there every Monday?"

"Yes." *Sometimes I go on Fridays too.*

"Jason Abbott and his family are not your responsibility." Henry took her arm. "There are some things we must discuss. The park is just down the way. We can sit on a bench and talk."

Ruth fell in step with him. "We could go home."

"The park is only two blocks from the bank." Henry quickened his pace. "This shouldn't take long."

Ruth wanted to ask so many questions. She kept her mouth shut.

They arrived at the park. A warm breeze stirred through the trees. Leaves littered the ground. Henry found a bench, dusted it with his handkerchief, sat down, and nodded toward the space beside him. "Sit down."

Ruth sat, feeling like a child about to be admonished by an elder. "Are you going to tell me I can no longer visit Jason and Clara?"

Henry stared into space. "Would it stop you?" Before she could answer, he added, "This has nothing to do with your friend Jason and his wife. It's about the ceremony that will stop this outrageous gossip. I have arranged for Reverend Marshall over in Hallettsville to perform our wedding ceremony next Thursday afternoon."

Ruth gasped. "That's Thanksgiving Day. Did you forget?"

Henry jerked his head in her direction. "Give me credit for knowing the day on which Thanksgiving falls."

His piercing stare and supercilious words had the intended effect. Sarcasm laced Ruth's voice. "Mrs. Murphy has spoken for a turkey from Mr. Elliott's poultry farm. I have planned a sumptuous dinner. What am I supposed to do with all that food?"

"Give it to some needy family." His voice gentled. "I want the children to be present for our wedding."

Ruth considered asking why, and decided against it. "What about Thanksgiving dinner? The children will be disappointed if we don't have one."

"There is a nice family restaurant in Hallettsville. I have made reservations for us to have dinner there." He stood. "I must go. I have a meeting in thirty minutes."

Ruth sat for a long time after Henry walked away, watching the wind-tossed leaves fall to the ground and chasing opposing thoughts around in her mind. The warm sun on her back was a reminder of passing time. She stood and stretched. Clara was expecting her.

Clara was waiting for her on the front porch. "I was afraid you weren't coming." She opened the screen door. "Do come in."

During her visit, Ruth explained she and her family would be out of town Thanksgiving Day. "It came as a surprise," she added. "Mr. Jarrett didn't tell me until today."

Clara clapped her hands. "I love surprises."

"So do I," Ruth said. "However, I do have one problem. I ordered a turkey from Mr. Elliott, and bought items that are perishable if not used by Thursday. I am hoping you will take them off my hands. It would be a shame for all that good food to go to waste. It's too late to cancel my order with Mr. Elliott."

Clara hesitated. "I don't know what Jason would say -- it would be nice to have a turkey for Thanksgiving."

"If Jason has a complaint, he can take it up with me." Ruth stood. "I will send the food over tomorrow. I'll call Mr. Elliott and explain that Jason will pick up the turkey Wednesday."

Ruth hurried home elated that she was able to give Clara and Jason a proper Thanksgiving dinner. She would also give Mrs. Murphy Wednesday, Thursday, and Friday off. The old biddy had a son who lived on the far side of the next county. Maybe she would like to visit him.

She found Mrs. Murphy at the kitchen drinking coffee and eating buttered biscuits with jelly. Ruth slid into the chair across from her. "I have good news."

Mrs. Murphy spread jelly on a biscuit. "There is coffee in the pot."

Ruth waved one hand. "No thank you. The good news is you are going to have a three day vacation." Ruth waited for an answer. When none was forthcoming, she added. "It will be paid. You will still receive your salary in full."

Mrs. Murphy asked, "When?"

"Wednesday, Thursday, and Friday."

Mrs. Murphy stared at Ruth in disbelief. "Nonsense, I can't take those days off. I plan to cook Thanksgiving dinner on Wednesday. I need to be here to serve it on Thursday. I will spend Friday getting the kitchen in order again."

"Forget about Thanksgiving dinner. Mr. Jarrett is taking the children and me on a short vacation." Ruth waited for some reaction from the other woman.

For several seconds silence reined. Ruth spoke again. "We will leave early Wednesday morning. We won't return until late Friday afternoon."

Mrs. Murphy laid her half-eaten biscuit in her plate. "What about the food you bought and the turkey you ordered?"

"I arranged for the turkey and the food to be given to a needy family. Everything is settled. Enjoy your three day vacation."

Mrs. Murphy drank the last of her coffee. "I could catch a bus over to visit my son and his family on Thanksgiving. Do you have Mr. Jarrett's permission to give me a three-day vacation?"

"I don't need his permission."

Mrs. Murphy reminded her, most unkindly, "I am Mr. Jarrett's employee. I will seek his permission before I go tearing off for three whole days."

This woman would try the patience of a saint. "Do that, meanwhile, I will I start my packing." Ruth hurried away before her anger burst its bonds and exploded into inflammatory words.

Chapter Ten

Cedar Gap, Texas
Thursday Morning
November 28th, 1917

Ruth put two suitcases on the floor board of the back seat of Henry's Model T. They were going to freeze riding all the way to Hallettsville in this open car. She bit her bottom lip to keep from complaining. That wouldn't be wise. Henry was already about as approachable as a bear with a sore head.

Henry stood beside his car with his crank in his hand. "Rosie will ride in front with me. You and the twins get in the back."

Jake howled, "No. I want to ride in front with you."

Joe followed suit. "So do I."

Rosie said, "It's all right, Papa. I don't mind if--"

Henry cut her short. "Get in the front seat and don't touch anything, just sit still and be quiet."

Rosie bowed her head, went around the car, and got into the front seat.

Henry was angry with Ruth and over nothing at all. That didn't give him leave to speak rudely to Rosie. The child was sensitive, and she adored Henry. Ruth herded the twins into the back seat. As soon as she got Henry alone, she would let him have it with both barrels.

Henry cranked the car until it sputtered to life. He hurried to get into the driver's seat. As he pulled out of the drive and onto the street, he glanced briefly in Rosie's direction. "I'm sorry, baby girl, for being so rude."

The words flew from Ruth's mouth before she could stop them. "You should be." She snuggled down into her heavy coat. This was not going to be a pleasant journey.

Much to Ruth's surprise, it was pleasant. They stopped at a quaint little café along the way and enjoyed a leisurely breakfast. Jake and Joe were on their best behavior, and Rosie, as always, conducted herself as an adult. How much she was like her mother, both in manner and appearance. *I will watch over her, Rachel, just as I promised.*

If she hoped to do that, she had best make peace with Henry. She had no idea he would react so violently when he learned she gave their Thanksgiving Day dinner to Jason and his family.

"How many times have I told you, Jason Abbott and his family are not your concern?"

His outburst kindled Ruth's answering rage. "*You told me to give the food to a needy family. That's what I did.*" From there things went from bad to worse.

"Ruth?" Henry's deep voice impinged on her wandering thoughts.

She pulled her mind back to the here and now. "Yes?"

"Your food has arrived." Henry lifted his knife and fork to slice the slab of ham on his plate.

Rosie folded her hands beneath her chin. "Not yet, Papa. We haven't said grace."

Jake and Joe followed suit by folding their hands beneath their chins and bowing their heads.

Henry's neck turned a ruddy red. That red found its way up and into his cheeks. He bowed his head and slanted a look in Ruth's direction. He didn't say a word, but she got the message. She bowed her head and said a short prayer asking God's blessings on the food set before them. The remainder of the meal, she dared not look Henry's direction.

"Aunt Ruth," Jake put his elbows on the table and smiled a smile aimed at melting Ruth's heart. It did. "Can we buy some of the cinnamon rolls to take with us?"

Rosie pointed. "They are over there, Aunt Ruth."

Ruth looked over her shoulder to see a display case filled with all kinds of tempting baked treats. "May we, and that's a great idea."

"I'll get them as I pay the bill." Henry stood and pushed his arms into the sleeves of his overcoat. "Get your coats on and get in the car."

Without a word in reply, the four of them exited the restaurant and got into the car.

Ruth decided, as Henry repeatedly turned the crank to start the car, that chilly weather and Model T Fords were not compatible.

Henry continued cranking until the motor gradually stirred to life. He jumped into the driver's seat and put the crank on the floorboard. "Blasted machine. The next time I buy a car it will have an electric starter."

Jake leaned forward in his seat. "What's an electric starter?"

Ruth wondered the same thing. She wasn't about to ask.

Joe echoed Jake's question. "Yeah, Papa. What is an electric starter?" He leaned so far forward he was almost breathing down Henry's neck.

Ruth tugged Joe's coat tail. "Sit back, boys."

Jake and Joe moved back as Henry explained, "In some of the newer cars the starter is in the floorboard. The driver can step on it and start the car."

Rosie asked, "Are we going to get a car like that?"

"Someday, but not anyway soon. This old Tin Lizzie is still in good shape."

All three children giggled at the name Tin Lizzie. After repeating

Tin Lizzy several times, Jake declared, "Our car has a name."

As they traveled, one by one, the children fell asleep. Joe first, then Rosie, and last of all, Jake.

Ruth wanted to discuss with Henry, their last disagreement. It wasn't a disagreement, it was a verbal free-for-all. Road noise made carrying on a serious conversation impossible. She must find a way to make peace with Henry, not for her sake, and certainly not for his. Rachel's children deserved a stable home through their growing up years. She knew what a deleterious effect an unhappy home could have on a child. She grew up in one. With renewed determination, she vowed, *I will carry out Rachel's last wish. The boys and my precious Pearl Rose will grow up in a stable, happy home.* There remained the problem of how to bring that about.

Chapter Eleven

Hallettsville, Texas
Wednesday Evening
November 28th, 1917

The sun had begun its westerly decline before the weary travelers reached Hallettsville. Henry drove to the center of town and stopped before an imposing two story brick structure bearing the impressive name of Fenwick Arms Hotel. A young man exited the lobby and came to stand beside Henry's Model T. "Good evening, Mr. Jarrett. Welcome to Fenwick Arms. We have been expecting you."

Ruth was impressed. Not many small towns in Texas could boast of having a hotel. Camp grounds, yes, tourists courts, maybe, but a hotel? "How long has this been here?"

Henry stepped from the car to the curb. "It opened last June. Get the children inside. I will see to our suitcases and the car."

The lobby was large and ornate. The furniture was Victorian, the lamps and chandelier elaborate. A grand piano stood to one side and near the entrance. *Someone mistook flamboyance for elegance.*

Jake and Joe ran from chair, to sofa, to chair, and onto another sofa, bouncing and laughing before they moved on to the next sofa or chair.

The look on the desk clerk's face was not a happy one. He said nothing.

Ruth explained, "They have been pent up in a car all day. They will settle down."

Rosie's face held awe. "This is the most beautiful place I ever saw. Look at that piano. May I touch it?"

Ruth nodded as she gave the desk clerk a look that threatened his demise if he objected. "Yes, you may."

"May I touch the keys?"

Ruth's stare never left the desk clerk's face "Yes, you may."

Henry coming through the lobby door stopped the boys in their tracks. They ceased the horseplay and sat, side by side, stiff and straight on a sofa.

Rosie stopped and looked back at her aunt. Ruth nodded her consent.

Rosie raced across the room and touched several keys, one at a time. She smiled when they made soft, tinkling sounds.

Ruth smiled too. Rosie was so delicately beautiful, just like her mother. Her sister had left her both a gift and a challenge. *I will care for her, and the boys, Rachel. Regardless of what comes or goes, I will find a way.*

The clerk handed Henry a ring holding three keys. "Your bags are in your rooms, sir." He pointed to the broad staircase to his right. "Up the stairs and turn left. Your rooms are numbers two-ten and two-twelve."

Henry took the keys from the desk clerk and called to his children, "Come along." He nodded to Ruth. "This way."

Ruth climbed the stairs, thinking as she went, that she had been remiss in not asking before she began this fool's journey, what the sleeping arrangements would be. The clerk *had* assigned them two rooms.

Henry unlocked room two-ten and opened the door. "You and Rosie will sleep here. The twins and I are in the next room. There is a door that adjoins our room to yours. The lock is on your side. If an emergency arises and you need me, you can call me. Lock your door when you get inside. Your bags are in your room. Good night."

Ruth followed Rosie into the room, and closed and locked the door. She was so weary her bones hummed with fatigue.

The room was large with two beds, two comfortable chairs, and a small table and two straight-back chairs in one corner.

Rosie stared upward. "I was hoping for chandeliers in here too. When I grow up, I will have a house with chandeliers in every room."

Ruth lifted a suitcase onto one of the beds. "May I come to visit you when you have that grand house?" She took Rosie's nightgown from the suitcase and pointed toward the door near the back wall. "Go bathe and change."

Rosie snagged the gown and hurried to the bathroom, saying over her shoulder as she went, "You must come and live with me. I would be unhappy if you were not near."

Ruth sat on the edge of the bed. *I would be unhappy without you, too, my dear little Pearl of great price.*

A recurring and darker thought crept into her mind. She must make peace with Henry, and she must do so before they said forever-binding wedding vows. An even more disturbing thought surfaced. She promised Rachel not only to care for her children, but also to see after her husband. In one revealing moment Ruth knew what she must do. She would surrender to being Henry's wife in every sense of the word. That idea was not at all repulsive. In many ways the anticipation of being with Henry was -- Her mind refused to admit what her heart was reluctant to own. *He's Rachel's husband. You are his unattractive sister-in-law, and nothing more.*

Rosie came from the bathroom with her clothes over her arm and her shoes held between the fingers of her other hand. "Our bathroom is Papa and Joe and Jake's bathroom too."

Ruth turned back the covers on one bed. "Are you sure?" She pointed to a chair. "Put your clothes on the chair, hop in bed, and I'll tuck you in."

Rosie obeyed and snuggled between the covers. "There's another door on the other side of the bathroom. Jake opened it and saw me in my night gown. He laughed and called me Mother Hubbard. Papa made him go away and told me to lock that door each time I came into the bathroom."

Ruth tucked the covers under Rosie's neck, and planted a kiss on her cheek. "Sweet dreams. I love you."

Rosie turned on her side. "Good night, Aunt Ruth. I love you too, bunches and bunches."

Ruth's fatigue receded as she planned a way to speak to Henry before tomorrow. She would wait until she was sure no one was in the bathroom, then she would invite Henry in for a talk. She searched inside her suitcase and found her gown and robe, and the book she was currently reading.

The Winning of Barbara Worth made her wish she could be as dainty and beautiful as the heroine of this story. *What you really want is to be like Rachel.* That thought had never occurred to her before. It was a disturbing one.

Two men pursued Barbara Worth. The only man to ever show the slightest interest in Ruth was Jason. That was long ago. He was a boy then, only eighteen-years-old. Looking back, Ruth had to confess, she did most of the pursuing.

She laid her book on the bed beside her, and stared into space as her mind wandered backward in time. Her mother's oft-spoken words rang in her ears. *Rachel got the beauty in the family, Ruth got the brains...*

Ruth shook her head as common sense kicked in. Time and experience had taught her the futility of wishing for what she could never have.

She hung her gown and robe over one arm. There was much to be done before she slept this night. First on the agenda was a bath.

The bathroom was tile and marble with intricate scrolls around the bathtub and along the walls. Ruth relaxed in a hot bath, rehearsing in her mind the speech she would make to Henry.

She would like to soak for hours, she knew she must get out, dress, and call Henry.

She dressed and stared into the mirror over the sink. Should she put her hair in a bun, or leave it cascading down her back? Making excuses would only postpone the inevitable. She ran a comb through her hair, tied the belt on her robe with a flourish, rapped, ever so lightly, on Henry's door, and waited for an answer.

The response was dead silence. She rapped again, this time with more force. Henry was coming to answer. She heard him stirring and moving on the other side.

He opened the door and squinted his eyes against the bathroom light. "What's the problem?"

The problems between them were many and complex. Should she begin to enumerate?" "I must speak with you, now, tonight."

For a moment she thought he might refuse. After a long pause and a longer sigh, he asked, "Where?"

Ruth pulled the door open wide and motioned, "In here. We will have some privacy."

Henry hesitated.

Ruth assured him, "It's important."

He squeezed through the door, and quickly closed it behind him.

Ruth gestured toward the commode. "Would you like to sit down?" She clasped her hands together to stop their shaking.

Henry sat. "What happened? You are as pale as a ghost."

Ruth perched on the side of the bathtub, and struggled to pull her scattered thoughts together. Her voice, her speech, and her good sense had deserted her. "It's, well. I--"

Henry put his hands on his knees and leaned forward. "For heaven's sake, woman, speak."

Chapter Twelve

Hallettsville, Texas
Wednesday Night
November 28th, 1917

Ruth found her voice and a smattering of courage. "You said the choice is mine. You said when I made my decision, I should tell you." She grimaced before hurrying to add, "I have, and I do."

Henry rubbed one cheek with his hand. "I have no idea what you are trying to tell me."

Maybe he didn't, and again, maybe he did. She decided to give him the benefit of a doubt. "I once asked you if when we married, would you expect me to carry out *all* my wifely duties. You said, the choice was mine. I have made my choice, and I do."

The garish bathroom light played across Henry's strong features and cast shadows across the wall behind him. He looked as if someone had delivered a blow to his midsection. "What brought on this sudden about face?"

"It is not sudden, I have thought about it for some time."

Henry questioned, "And?"

"I want the children to have a happy, secure home." Ruth ran her hand along the rim of the bathtub and stared at the tiles on the floor.

Henry repeated, "And?"

Ruth's head came up as her patience snapped. "I promised Rachel I would take care of you and her children." She stopped. "What I am trying to say is--" What was she trying to say? She knew all too well, and there was no refined way to say it. "I know men have needs. As your wife it is my duty--"

Henry catapulted to his feet, and stared down at her, his eyes blazing blue fire. "There is a name for women who bargain with their bodies, and it's not a pretty one."

Was that what he believed? That thought made her sick inside. Her chin lifted. "Is that what you think I am doing?"

He asked softly, "Isn't it?"

Ruth stood and met his heated stare. Where was the answering anger that saw her through all confrontational situations? It had disappeared along with her self-respect. "I never thought of it that way." She owed this man an apology. "I'm sorry. I can see now, I was wrong."

Henry sat once more on the lid of the commode and dropped his head into his hands. "How little you understand." He lifted his face to stare at her. "I want a wife who comes to me because of her needs, not mine. I want it to be because she cares, not because of some misplaced sense of duty."

She had hurt him, and in so doing, wounded herself. "I didn't mean what I said in the way you assumed I did. Please forgive me."

He stood, this time very slowly. "I apologize for my atrocious behavior. It's not flattering for a man's soon-to-be wife to admit that she -- Let's wipe the slate clean, and start anew."

Ruth wanted to ask how they went about starting anew, considering their long and unpleasant history. It would be best to save that for a more convenient time. "Good night, Henry."

"Good night, Ruth."

*****

Hallettsville, Texas, Thursday Morning, November 29th, 1917

Ruth slept fitfully and woke early. She dressed quickly. Her hopes were high when she chose a dress for today. It was a lovely ivory color trimmed with ecru lace. It had a wide cape collar, three-quarter length sleeves, a dropped waist, and a skirt with floating panels. In a few short sentences, she had destroyed those hopes and turned her love for the dress into utter dislike. She would wear it today, she had no choice. It was the only dress she brought. She would never wear it again.

Should she tell Henry she couldn't marry him? *And break your promise to Rachel?* Rachel would understand, and be glad Ruth had the intelligence to refuse what would bring nothing but unhappiness to two people she loved. *Suppose then Henry marries someone else? That would put my beloved niece and nephews in the hands of some strange stepmother.* She would lose them. Panic traveled up from Ruth's stomach and lodged in her throat. "I can't let that happen."

A bang on the door and Henry calling "Ruth," made her jump and catch her breath.

Rosie sat up in bed and rubbed her eyes. "Is it time to get up?"

Ruth nodded, "Yes, dear, it is. Get dressed. Your new things are in the bathroom. Don't forget to lock both doors."

Henry knocked again. "Ruth, will you answer the door?"

Rosie headed for the bathroom.

What did Henry want now? Nothing good from the strength of his knock and the tone of his voice. Ruth opened the door.

Henry stood on the other side, looking magnificently handsome in his white shirt and his gray flannel pants with deep center creases and wide turned up cuffs. Without preamble, he announced, "Jake refuses to wear a tie."

Ruth stood staring at the man before her. Why had she not noticed before how incredibly handsome he was?

Henry asked, "Are you no longer speaking to me?"

Ruth stepped around him and into the room. "What about Joe?"

Henry stood holding onto the door knob. "I haven't asked him yet."

You don't ask six-year-olds, you tell them. Ruth approached Joe and held out her hand. "Give me your, tie, Joe, and stand."

Joe obeyed and stood and faced his aunt.

Ruth draped the tie around his neck and began the process of tying it. "You are going to look so handsome, and so grown-up in your new tie." She completed the knot and gave it a pat. "I am proud of you for being so grown-up."

She dropped a kiss on Joe's cheek before retracing her footsteps back toward the door.

"What about me?" Jake howled.

Ruth turned. "What about you?"

"Are you going to tie my tie?"

"Do you want me to?" Poor baby, he looked so sad, but he needed to learn.

Jake sniffed. "I want to look handsome and grown-up like Joe."

Ruth knelt before the child and took him in her arms. "Being handsome and grown-up is not only how you look, but also how you behave."

An impish smile crawled across Jake's face. "If I promise to behave, will you tie my tie, Aunt Ruth?"

That impish grin melted her heart. Ruth tied Jake's tie and kissed his cheek. "Now I have two gentlemen to be proud of."

Joe tugged at her skirt. "What about Papa? Is he a gentleman?"

Ruth caught Henry's glance and held it. "Your papa is a fine gentleman."

Rosie came through the door and stood beside her father. "Look, Papa, at my new dress. Aunt Ruth bought it for me." She turned toward her aunt. "Aunt Ruth, will you do my hair?"

Ruth followed Rosie through the door, telling Henry, as she passed him, "Knock when you are ready to go."

Ruth combed Rosie's long, dark curls, pulled the side curls to the crown of her head, and tied them with a huge pink ribbon that matched the pink velvet dress she wore. "You look beautiful."

Rosie asked, "Do I look like a lady?"

Ruth's heart overflowed with love for this little girl. "You look like your mother, and you are a lady."

"Can I look like my mother, and *be* like you, and still be a lady?"

Those words slammed into Ruth with the force of a body blow. Even a child could see the difference between Ruth and her dead sister. Rachel *was* a lady, modest and sweet, and smooth-tempered. Ruth was none of those things. *Rosie wants to be like me?* Ruth searched her brain for some answer, and didn't find one.

Henry banged on the door. "We are ready. Meet us outside."

Ruth breathed a sigh of relief. "Put on your coat, it's time to go."

Rosie pushed her arms through her coat sleeves. "Are we going to eat in a restaurant now?"

Ruth buttoned her niece's coat. "Yes, we will have our Thanksgiving dinner there."

Rosie took Ruth's hand. "Looking elegant and eating in a restaurant is going to be so much fun."

Ruth squeezed Rosie's hand before letting it go. She slipped her arms into her own coat. Was "fun" too much to hope for? *Please, God, don't let it be a disaster.*

Chapter Thirteen

Hallettsville, Texas
Noon, November 29th, 1917

The restaurant Henry chose was even more plush and ornate than the Fenwick Arms Hotel. As they entered, Henry took her arm. "We will be dining in a private dining room. Perhaps I should have consulted you first. I didn't and now the deed is done."

Ruth could make that statement about so many things. "A private room will be nice. For a small town, Hallettsville has many luxurious amenities."

"It's a tourist town. During late spring and summer the town brims over with vacationers."

A distinguished looking waiter came toward them. "Mr. Jarrett?"

Henry nodded.

"This way." He led them to a room resplendent with ornate furnishings. A gleaming chandelier hung overhead.

Rosie clapped her hands. "This is a splendid dining room."

Indeed it was. The glowing mahogany table was set for five. The matching chairs were padded with a heavy, intricately designed fabric.

Joe and Jake stared at the splendor around them. Joe's "Wow" accompanied Jake's "Gee whiz."

With the waiter's assistance, they were soon seated.

The meal was served in courses. With each succeeding course, Ruth was more uncomfortable. This dinner must be costing Henry a mint. Over coffee and a delicious slice of pumpkin pie, she broached a subject she had long wanted to discuss with her soon-to-be husband. "I would like to take over the running of the household. I'm sure you have a household budget. I would like to oversee it."

Henry's fork stopped halfway to his mouth. "If that's what you wish. May I ask why?"

Ruth pushed her dessert plate with its half-eaten slice of pie from her. "Our meals are neither balanced nor nutritious. They should be both. With your permission, in the future they will be."

Henry shrugged. "As you wish, my dear."

Rosie had listened to their short conversation with rapt attention. She turned to her brothers who sat across from her. "Papa called Aunt Ruth dear. See, I told you."

Ruth was careful to keep her voice casual. Her heart picked up an uneven beat. "What did you tell your brothers?"

"I told them now we were going to have two mamas, one in heaven, and one on earth."

Henry pressed his napkin to his lips as coffee spewed from his mouth. When he could get his breath he sputtered, "How -- Who -- I don't--"

Ruth came to his rescue, although she wondered why she bothered. "You have only one mama. She's in heaven. Even after I marry your papa, I will remain your aunt."

Jake wailed, "That's not fair. How come Papa can have you for a wife and we can't have you for a mama?"

Would she ever learn to think before she spoke? Ruth looked toward Henry. His grin said, *talk yourself out of this one.* When he spoke it was to the children. "Aunt Ruth can be your substitute mama until you go to heaven to be with your real mama."

Joe turned his head to one side. "Can we call her Aunt Mama until we get to heaven?"

Henry beamed at his son. "You must ask Aunt Ruth about that."

In chorus, the children begged, "Please, Aunt Ruth, say yes."

What could Ruth say? "Yes, but only if your papa agrees."

Rosie held up one dainty hand to silence her brothers. "Please say yes, Papa, then Joe and Jake and I will have a mama, just like everyone else at church and school."

Henry nodded his approval. "Yes."

Ruth's bubble of happiness burst. She was not someone special to them. Their concern was to have a mama. Any mama would do. She touched her napkin to her lips before putting it on the table. "We should go. The minister is waiting."

During the short drive to Reverend Marshall's home, the children discussed the events of yesterday and today, sometimes all talking at once. Suddenly Rosie slapped her hand over her mouth and pulled it away slowly. "We forgot to say grace before we had that yummy Thanksgiving Day dinner. Do you think God will punish us?"

Ruth must set them straight on this issue, here and now. "We are God's children. He loves us. He doesn't punish us because we forget."

Jake, as ever the devil's advocate, asked, "What does He punish us for?"

Over Henry's chuckle, Ruth replied, "He doesn't punish us. When we do things we know we shouldn't, He lets us suffer the consequences of our wrongdoings. It's called learning from our mistakes."

Joe narrowed his eye in his brother's direction. "It's like when you put Hattie Jenkin's pigtail in your inkwell, and had to sit on a stool by Miss Ames's desk and wear a dunce cap the rest of the day."

The two boys collapsed in giggles.

Henry pulled to the front of a stately old plantation style home. "We're here. Enough of this foolishness, boys. This is a solemn occasion."

Reverend Marshall was an imposing figure, tall, thin, and with a distinguished air about him that declared him to be someone of importance. He shook Henry's hand and welcomed him warmly before turning to Ruth. "This must be your bride. Do come inside, all of you."

Henry made introductions. "She is indeed. Meet Miss Ruth Garland, and these are my children, Pearl Rose, Joseph, and Jacob." He stood back to let the others step inside.

The house was as stately and imposing as the gentleman who lived in it. Rosie's face glowed. "Reverend Marshall, your home is beautiful."

Reverend Marshall looked down at her. "No more beautiful that you are, my child."

Rosie blushed. "Thank you, sir."

Jake stepped to Joe's side. "My brother and I are twins. Can you tell?"

The two looked nothing alike, Joe was hefty and tall for his age. Jake was skinny and short. Their facial features where nothing alike. Joe would someday be a handsome man. Jake's pixie features showed character. Manly beauty would always elude him. Ruth stepped in before things got out of hand. "Shall we get on with what we came here for?" She pointed to a long couch near the fireplace. "Sit there, children, and behave."

For once, all three obeyed.

Reverend Marshall performed a short, but touching ceremony. Ruth was so caught-up in the silver-tongued grandeur of his words she forgot her uncertainties and relaxed.

"With this ring I thee wed--" Henry's slipping a wide gold band on the third finger of her left hand, brought Ruth back to reality with a jolt. She stood tense and waiting to say the two short words that would forever bind her to a man who could never love her. *I will make it work. I have to, for the sake of Rachel and her children.*

Reverend Marshall's deep-toned voice penetrated her wandering thoughts. "Miss Garland?"

Ruth's mind, along with her resolve returned to the unfolding ceremony. "I do, yes, I do."

Reverend Marshall smiled. "By the power vested in me by the State of Texas and the Risen Savior, I now pronounce you man and wife. You may kiss your bride."

Ruth closed her eyes, and waited. Henry's kiss was little more than a peck. It confirmed what she had long suspected. Henry did not find her physically attractive. She opened her eyes and concealed her hurt behind a smile.

Jake jumped from his seat. "Hurrah, we have an Aunt Mama." He dashed across the room to give both Henry and Ruth a hug.

Ruth wanted to leave this place, and the sooner, the better. A block of sadness gathered in her stomach, and wedged there. This should be the happiest day of her life. Remorse was all she felt.

The last goodbye was finally said, and they drove back toward the hotel. Henry stopped before a store with a sign over it that read, *Joe's Ice Cream Parlor.* "Would you look at this? Joe, I didn't know you owned an ice cream parlor. Shall we have a sundae here?"

Joe squealed with delight. "Is this really my place?"

"No, stupid," Jake replied. "This belongs to some grown-up Joe."

Rosie came to Joe's defense. "You are not stupid, Joe. Jake is just jealous."

"Am not." Jake shot back.

"Are too," Joe said before asking, "May we have a sundae here?"

For the first time since Reverend Marshall pronounced them man and wife, Henry looked at his bride. "Ruth?"

The place looked like a decent enough establishment. It would be a welcome change from the fancy restaurant where they had Thanksgiving Dinner. "Get out, kids. This afternoon we eat sundaes at *Joe's Ice Cream Parlor.*"

Chapter Fourteen

Cedar Gap, Texas
Tuesday
December 4th, 1917

Monday afternoon, after the Friday she, Henry, and the children returned from Hallettsville, Ruth relieved Mrs. Murphy of all her duties except the cooking of meals and keeping the house in order. Hereafter Ruth would be purchasing all groceries and supplies for the kitchen, she would also be planning all menus, and paying all current bills. She asked for the statements from last month, and for records of past household accounts.

Mrs. Murphy was beyond indignant. She told Ruth she kept no such records. She bought what she needed, and sent the bills to Mr. Jarrett.

Ruth let it go at that. What else could she do? For a man who dealt in finances, Henry was terribly remiss about his own accounts.

Monday evening, after she got the children to bed, Ruth went to Henry's office. Her intention was to talk with him about the situation with Mrs. Murphy.

With a wave of his hand, Henry dismissed her before she could begin to explain, calling it a tempest in a teapot and reminding her of her request to be allowed to manage the household. "Take care of it as you see fit."

Ruth's resolve to be tolerant and understanding disappeared like smoke in the wind. "Rest assured, I will." She stormed from the room, slamming the door behind her.

Tuesday morning Ruth intercepted the bill from Elliott's Poultry Farm. They charged her for two turkeys. Something was amiss.

Ruth walked the children to school before going directly to Clara's.

Clara greeted her at the door with Jasper on her hip, and Leon hanging onto her skirt. "Come in. Coffee is ready."

Ruth stayed only long enough to ask if Jason got the turkey from Mr. Elliott's farm on the Wednesday before Thanksgiving.

Clara assured her that he picked it up early Wednesday morning, "and a fine turkey it was." She asked if there was a problem. *That is what I intend to find out.* "No problem. I will see you Friday."

Ruth went home and called Elliott's Poultry Farm.

Mr. Elliott told her Mrs. Murphy's son picked up the second turkey late Wednesday afternoon.

Ruth thanked him, and hung up the telephone. She had places to go and people to see before the day was done.

She spent the morning and much of the afternoon visiting grocery, dry goods, department, and drug stores. Each place told the same story. They didn't have itemized accounts of what Mr. Jarrett's housekeeper purchased each month. They kept tally of the amount spent each month. At the beginning of the next month, they sent Mr. Jarrett a bill, which he promptly paid.

At each store Ruth left explicit instructions. She, his wife, was the sole person with the authority to charge anything to Mr. Jarrett's account. The manager of the department store was reluctant. He would need Mr. Jarrett's approval to make such a change.

Ruth's temper flared. "Close the account," she snapped. "Hereafter I will order from the Sears Roebuck Catalogue."

The manager reconsidered and apologized. "It will be as you wish, Mrs. Jarrett."

Being addressed as Mrs. Jarrett put out the fire of Ruth's anger. "See that it is." She turned and walked from the store.

That evening, after she heard the children's prayers, and tucked each one in bed, she returned to stand once again at the door of Henry's office. She knocked and waited.

A belligerent, "Yes," sounded from the other side.

"It's me, Ruth, may I come in?"

"If you must."

Why else would I waste my time knocking? "I must." She came inside, shut the door, and stood facing him. "I have some things to tell you."

Henry sat behind his desk, reading a book. He closed it, being careful to mark his place. "Sit down."

Ruth dragged a chair across the room and placed it in front of Henry's desk. She was not going to broadcast her news across the room. "I am going to fire Mrs. Murphy." She waited for his scathing reply.

It never came, instead, he asked, oh, so softly, "Am I allowed to ask why?"

Ruth clasped her hand together, and leaned forward to put them on his desk. "She is stealing from you. I have no idea how long it has been going on."

"How did you come by this knowledge?" Henry's expression was unreadable. He rubbed his chin with his thumb and forefinger.

"She charged two turkeys from Elliott's Poultry farm on Thanksgiving."

Henry put his hands over hers. "You opened my mail?"

He made it sound as if Ruth was the culprit. "Just the bill from Elliott's Farm. I thought since I was taking over the reins of the household--"

Henry's hands tightened around hers. "I had several calls from local stores this afternoon."

Ruth pulled her hands free and dropped them into her lap. "I was checking to see if Mrs. Murphy ran up more bills."

Henry's words fell like tossed pebbles out into the silence of the room "I gave the turkey to Mrs. Murphy as a gift. I knew her son was coming for Thanksgiving."

Ruth lifted her head. "I thought she was going to his home. She said something about catching a bus."

Henry shook his head from side to side. "Her son decided it would be better if he and his family came to Mrs. Murphy. He disliked the idea of her traveling so far alone."

Ruth felt like a fool. "Why didn't you tell me?"

Henry came to stand beside her chair. "It never occurred to me that I should."

Ruth closed her eyes and sighed. "I was so sure -- I am so sorry. Go ahead, yell at me. I deserve it."

Henry took her hands and pulled her to her feet. "I owe you an apology also." His hands were warm, his voice comforting. "I know you were acting in what you thought to be my best interest. Hereafter, I shall try to be more gentle and understanding."

Harshness and sarcasm Ruth could have fought against. Gentleness and what could pass for affection, she had no defense. She was left with nothing but a clear picture of her malicious behavior. She was beginning to see why her sister loved this man so dearly. *He loved her just as dearly. He still does.* She stepped back. "I am the one who should apologize to you, and to Mrs. Murphy." She pulled her hands free. "I am sorry, Henry. Please forgive me."

Henry smiled at her. That smile did strange things to her heart rate. "There is nothing to forgive. You thought you were protecting your husband."

Ruth breathed a sigh of relief. "Thank you. I will apologize to Mrs. Murphy in the morning." She turned to go.

Henry called after her, "Perhaps we should set aside a time each evening to talk."

Ruth liked that idea. "I could come to your office each evening after I tuck the children in bed."

Henry sat, once again, behind his desk. "I look forward to those meetings."

Ruth opened the door. "So do I." *Much more than you know.* She closed the door, and walked down the hall. She and Henry would be talking each evening. Anxiety moved in around her elation. Tomorrow morning she must apologize to Mrs. Murphy. She was about to make a person who barely tolerated her into someone who hated her.

She vented her frustrations in a letter to Flossie before preparing for bed. Flossie got an earful this time.

As Ruth knelt beside her bed, like an epiphany, the revelation came. Her prayers each night were little more than a ritual. She said the same empty words, and made the same hollow requests, with little thought of the might and power of the God to whom she prayed. A scripture from one of the Apostle Paul's epistles ran through her mind. *Having a form of Godliness, but denying the power thereof... (Second Timothy, 3:5 KJV)*

She bowed her head, and for the first time since her mother died, really prayed, instead of reciting lifeless words. She humbly entreated for wisdom and guidance. "Forgive me, Father, for the many ways I have failed you. Give me wisdom to care for Rachel's children. Show me the way to be a good wife to Henry. Give me patience and compassion. Teach me not to be judgmental and critical. I ask these things in the precious name of my Lord and Savior, Christ Jesus."

She crawled into bed, and snuggled beneath the covers. How could she have been so blind as not to see her own faults and shortcomings? Sweet peace stole over her. Despite all her faults and shortcomings, God loved her. With that comforting assurance, she drifted into a dreamless sleep.

Chapter Fifteen

Cedar Gap, Texas
Wednesday Morning
December 5th, 1917

Ruth woke the next morning with a sense of impending dread. She had to apologize to Mrs. Murphy. She went downstairs and placed Flossie's letter atop a stack of outgoing mail before speaking to the woman who stood beside the stove, stirring the contents of an iron skillet. "Good morning."

"Mornin'," Mrs. Murphy replied before adding, "Mr. Jarrett left a message for you. He said I should tell you because of the cold weather, he got the children up early, and drove them to school." Her words were clipped and terse.

Ruth took a cup from the cabinet. "I owe you an apology. I spoke out of turn yesterday morning. I knew too little and assumed too much. Please forgive me." She heaved a long sigh. *There, I said it.*

Mrs. Murphy's jaw dropped before snapping shut. She swallowed, and asked, "Would you like a cup of coffee?"

"I would, thank you."

Mrs. Murphy waved her spatula toward the table. "Sit down, unless you plan to drink it standing in the middle of the kitchen floor."

Ruth sat, unsure how she should react.

Mrs. Murphy poured coffee in Ruth's cup. "I'll fetch your breakfast." She brought scrambled eggs, biscuits, and bacon, and set the plate before Ruth. "There's jam on the table."

Ruth asked, "Would you like to have a cup of coffee with me?"

"Don't mind if I do." Mrs. Murphy poured her coffee and sat across from Ruth. "It's cold outside. If you will make a list, I can fetch the groceries for the week. I buy on Wednesday because that's the day the fresh meat comes in. I thought maybe--" She stopped.

Mrs. Murphy couldn't buy a penny stick of candy, Ruth had seen to that. "Maybe we could plan the week's menu and then go together, if that's all right with you." Was this Ruth Garland asking her housekeeper's permission to tag along with her as she shopped? No, she was Mrs. Henry Jarrett, wife and mother. It was time she acted like an adult.

Mrs. Murphy took a sip of coffee. "We can learn a lot from each other."

Ruth took that as a yes. "Let's get started."

Mrs. Murphy pointed to Ruth's half-filled plate. "Eat your breakfast first."

Ruth pushed the plate aside. "Later."

Mrs. Murphy stood. "I'll get paper and pencils."

*****

Cedar Gap, Texas
Friday Evening
December 14th, 1917

Ruth knocked on Henry's office door and waited. She looked forward to her evening conversations with him. Over the past ten days they had settled some matters that hindered peace in the household. Ruth's apology to, and acceptance of, Mrs. Murphy, took away much of the stress that permeated the house. Ruth was learning discord, though not visible, was felt by all those who lived where it existed.

Henry ceased to complain about Ruth's weekly visits to Clara's. There existed between them an uneasy truce. Ruth knew their edgy harmony depended heavily on her keeping her temper. She vowed to do that. So far, she had.

Henry called, "Come in."

Ruth opened the door and stepped inside.

Henry sat, as always, behind his desk. "It's good to see you, my dear."

Ruth had ambivalent feelings about him calling her dear. Was it intended as a term of endearment, or was it a reflexive action? After all, she was his wife. *No, you are not. At least, not in any true sense of the word.* "Good evening, Henry." She sat in the chair that now had a permanent place in front of his desk. "It is time we made some plans for Christmas."

"I agree." Henry stared at her over tented fingers. "I made arrangements for a tree. It will be delivered and erected in the front parlor next Wednesday. The children will be out of school for the holidays that afternoon. Decorating the tree and the house will give them something enjoyable to do between then and Christmas Day."

Ruth was pleased by his thoughtfulness. "I plan to take them Christmas shopping Thursday."

They sat in awkward silence until Henry asked, "Did you have a pleasant day?"

"Not completely. I have a friend whose husband is in a hospital in France. I had a letter from her today. Her husband has been seriously injured. She is worried that he may lose his left leg."

Henry's brow wrinkled. "I am sorry to hear that."

The war had raged across Europe since June, with battle after bloody battle. Ruth had never discussed the war with Henry. "Will this conflict ever be over?"

Henry's complacent answer angered her. "In time, my dear. Have a little patience."

Ruth's vow to hold onto her temper slipped away on wings of indignation. "Patience? I am to be patient while the Eastern Front disintegrates into a civil war between the Russians, and the Western Front turns into a bloody massacre with American soldiers being killed and maimed by the hundreds? Meanwhile women in this country are arrested and sent to jail for demanding their right to vote? I--"

Henry held up one hand. "Step down from your soap box. I get your message."

Ruth slumped in her chair. "It seems all I do is apologize. Again, I am sorry." She sat up and gripped the arms of her chair. "I am passionate about hating war and fighting injustice."

"I would say you are also opinionated." For a moment the ghost of a smile played around Henry's lips. He sobered. "I had no idea you kept so abreast of current events."

Ruth refused to meet his gaze. "Can we talk about something else?"

Henry leaned back in his chair. "Like what?"

"Like I want to buy gifts for Jason and Clara's children." Ruth sat on the edge of her seat, and waited. After a short span of silence, she added, "I will use my own money."

"You bring up a subject that has troubled me for some time," Henry said. "The monthly interest from your father's estate is practically nothing. Why have you never asked me about a personal allowance?"

He was moving toward a place Ruth didn't wish to go, not with Henry. "My father had no estate. He did own the house Mama and I lived in. When Mama died and Rachel sold it, she said I should let you handle the proceeds, and I did. I spent the bulk of it paying my tuition for nursing school."

Henry rubbed his chin with his thumb and forefinger. "That's not what I asked. Since we are on the subject, we should come to an understanding. Each month, I will place twenty-five dollars in your account. That should supply you with wardrobe and pin money needs."

Ruth didn't spend twenty-five dollars a year on clothes. Pin money? Her only extravagance was buying an occasional second-hand book. She sat, literally speechless.

Henry continued on in that same matter-of-fact tone. "The Mayor's Christmas Ball is next Friday. You can buy a new gown and shoes for the event. Rachel looked forward to this occasion with a great deal of anticipation. Her jewelry is in a safe-deposit box at the bank. Come in next Wednesday afternoon and we can go through it. Perhaps you will find something to wear to the ball."

Once again, Ruth's anger caught fire. She smothered it with a strong force of will. "I would not feel comfortable wearing Rachel's jewelry."

Henry's eyebrows lifted before lowering to meet in a frown. "I misspoke. I should have said your jewelry. Rachel requested before she died that you have it."

Why hadn't he told her before? An insidious thought snaked through her brain. She stared down at the wide gold band on the third finger of her left hand. *Did it once belong to Rachel? Was she wearing a second-hand wedding ring?*

A muscle flicked along Henry's jaw. "Your wedding band did not belong to Rachel. I bought it especially for you. It reminded me of you. The jewelry in the box is not worth a king's ransom, only a string of pearls, a diamond ring, and a cameo broach, along with Rachel's wedding band, and her engagement ring." His eyes met hers.

She saw there hurt and an emotion she couldn't define. "I would like to leave the jewelry for Rachel's children. The wedding ring should go to one of the twins, the engagement ring to the other. The pearls, the cameo, and the diamond ring should go to Rosie. When she grows to be a woman, she will treasure them."

Henry nodded. "As you wish. Enjoy shopping for your finery to wear to the Mayor's Ball."

Ruth stood. "Good night, Henry."

"Good night, Ruth."

Chapter Sixteen

Cedar Gap, Texas
Monday Afternoon
December 17th, 1917

Ruth had little interest in shopping for a dress to wear to the Mayor's Ball. She had no fashion sense, and little awareness in the latest styles. She was reluctant to dress in finery and parade around among a strutting bevy of painted petite beauties. She decided to find something unpretentious, something with few frills and no beads. She walked the children to school before heading toward town and Miss Millie's Ladies Boutique.

Miss Millie opened the door as Ruth stepped under the store's awning. "Good morning, Miss Garland, excuse me, Mrs. Jarrett. What brings you out so early in the day?" She stepped aside. "Do come in."

Ruth came inside and stood, waiting for her eyes to adjust to the dimness. "Good morning, Miss Millie. I have come to shop for evening wear."

Miss Millie tucked her lace handkerchief into her sleeve. "My, how time does fly. It seems only yesterday your mother was bringing you in to buy you dresses for school."

Reminiscences crept from the crevasses of Ruth's mind, bringing memories she had rather not recall. "I remember." Her mother's words echoed through her mind. *"I do hope you have something age-appropriate for a ten-year-old child who is taller than her mama." Grace Garland emitted a rippling titter of laughter. "Just so long as she doesn't grow as tall as her papa."*

Miss Millie pointed toward the rear of the shop. "The evening wear is in the back. I have fewer calls for it these days, what with the war, and the drought. Will you also need shoes and an evening wrap?"

Ruth followed Miss Millie to the back of the boutique. "I will need all of those, and also an evening bag. Mr. Jarrett is taking me to the Mayor's Ball next Friday evening."

Miss Millie clapped her hands together. "How exciting. You will also need a dancing corset."

Ruth skidded to a stop. "A what?"

Miss Millie didn't slow her pace. "A dancing corset, my dear. They are less restrictive than regular corsets. You will have room to move about more freely when you dance."

Ruth hadn't worn a corset since her high school graduation. She wore one then because of Rachel's ultimatum that she most assuredly *would* dress appropriately for her graduation. She pulled her thoughts back to the present. "I didn't know there was such a thing as a dancing corset."

"They are the latest rage." Miss Millie stopped before a rack of evening dresses. "The larger sizes are toward the back." She took from the rack a gown made of pink taffeta and light blue crepe with a white lace overlay and glass bead decorations. "Isn't this lovely? The latest fashion is to combine contrasting colors and textures."

Ruth shuttered. "It's not my style. I want something plain, but elegant."

Miss Millie snapped her fingers. "I have just the thing. Stay here. I'll go in the store room and get it." She returned a few minutes later carrying an ivory satin dress with a black velvet collar. The three-quarter length sleeves were cuffed with black velvet. A wide band of black velvet adorned the hem of the flowing paneled, ankle-length skirt. The only other decoration was a wide velvet sash. It was exactly what Ruth hoped to find. "I'll take it. I need an evening wrap too."

Miss Millie hung the dress on a high wall hanger. "This is your lucky day, and mine too, I must say. The dress is a part of an ensemble. There is a matching long evening cape of black velvet lined with ivory satin, and a lovely black bag with the same matching ivory lining."

She turned and was almost to the back door before Ruth's cry of "Wait," stopped her. As she turned, Ruth asked, "How much?"

"It's half price." Miss Millie disappeared through the door.

Ruth perched on the most substantial looking chair in the room, and waited. Miss Millie hadn't sold this lovely dress, not because of its style, but because of its length and size. Should she be pleased or annoyed? Before she had time to decide, Miss Millie reappeared carrying a black cloak randomly adorned with tiny ivory satin bows, and a black velvet evening bag with an ivory satin lining and a large ivory tassel hanging from its bottom. "Would you like to try on these lovely garments?"

Ruth came away from Miss Millie's having purchased, not only the gown-cloak-bag evening ensemble, but also a pair of black pumps with Louie heels, a peacock feather fan, a pair of ivory kidskin gloves, and yes, a dancing corset. She got all these at a bargain price, only fifteen dollars and fifty seven cents. That included delivery. She paid for them with her own money. Miss Millie promised that everything would be delivered before noon tomorrow.

*****

Cedar Gap, Texas
Thursday Evening
December 20th, 1917

Ruth knocked on Henry's office door and heard his brooding, "Enter." Henry was not a man who hid his emotions well. Through dinner he was like a pouting child, silent and withdrawn, speaking only when he was spoken to. She didn't know why, but she was sure she was about to find out.

She opened the door and came inside. "Good evening, Henry."

Henry was not in his usual seat behind his desk. He stood at the side of the room with his hands behind his back, staring at her with the strangest look in his eyes.

Ruth sat in the chair near his desk and dealt with the situation the only way she knew how, by facing it head-on. "Are you going to say good evening, or does the lecture start now?"

Henry shook his head from side to side. "I thought we had an agreement. You purchased several items from *Miss Millie's Boutique* for a ridiculously low price and paid cash for them. Why didn't you charge them to your personal account?" His voice was stern and touched with aching hurt.

He caught her completely off-guard. Ruth stammered "T-they w-were on sale. How did you know?"

"I made it my business to find out." He drew a long breath, "Ruth, you don't have to look for bargain merchandise. Buy what you like. You can return your first purchases tomorrow, and buy anything that catches your fancy. This time use money from your personal account."

His act of kindness was touching, but misplaced. In his attempt to be generous, he called into question her taste in clothing, under minded her belief in herself, and fed her worst fear. She was not good enough to be the wife of Henry Jarrett. She hid her pain behind a benign smile. "You are most kind. I will take care of it tomorrow."

Henry came to sit in the chair behind his desk. "I have arranged for Mrs. Murphy to stay with the children Friday night. After the first of the year I insist you find a live-in nursemaid to help you with them."

Ruth was set to tell him she didn't need a nursemaid's help. She couldn't. *Good heavens, I have great affection for this man who is doing his best to be considerate and thoughtful.* "I will do that, thank you."

The next morning, Ruth walked the children to school and hurried to Miss Millie's. She wanted to catch the delivery man before he began his rounds. As she waited for Miss Millie to open the store, she pondered over what she would wear to the ball. Maybe Miss Millie has a skirt long enough for her. *I can decorate one of my blouses. My regular coat will have to do.*

Miss Millie opened the door. "Come in, Mrs. Jarrett. I have been expecting you."

Ruth came inside. Belatedly, Miss Millie's words registered. "You were expecting me? Why?"

"I am afraid I have bad news? You see--"

Ruth didn't see. That was the problem. "I'm afraid I don't."

"I can't take back the merchandise you bought yesterday. Items on sale are not returnable. It's a hard and fast rule. I hope you understand--"

Ruth waved one hand. Now she did understand. Miss Millie had sold her a white elephant. She wasn't about to take it back. "It's all right, Miss Millie. Rules are rules." *I will wear my ensemble, and hope for the best.* "I would like to look for some day dresses." Since Henry insisted she spend his money, she would be happy to oblige him.

Miss Millie let out a whistling sigh of relief. "You are most gracious. Thank you for understanding. The things you bought should arrive at your home around noon. Let me show you some dresses that have just arrived from New York City."

Ruth left the store feeling happy about Miss Millie's "rule". She could wear her relatively plain dress to the ball, and be lost in the bevy of beauties who were sure to attend.

Chapter Seventeen

Cedar Gap, Texas
Friday Evening
December 21st, 1917

Ruth was fortunate. The dress she bought fit to perfection, so did the shoes. She dressed with care. The dancing corset was not so bad after all. She dusted face powder across her nose in an effort to cover her freckles. Next she applied a touch of lipstick, and tied her hair atop her head with a ribbon. It hung to her shoulders in curls. She had never dared wear it that way before. It made her appear taller. *Appear?* With her hair style and wearing her Louie heels, she was six feet. She put on her gloves, draped her cloak around her shoulders, grabbed her bag and fan, and hurried toward the stairs.

Henry stood at the foot of the stairway. He stared as she came down the steps. "My dear, you look like a goddess."

Ruth swallowed her surprise. "Thank you."

He held out both his hands. "You are beautiful". He wore a black, cutaway coat with tails. His pants matched his coat. His shirt was white and his bow tie black. His feet were shod in black patent leather pumps. His spats were grey with pearl buttons. He was so handsome he took her breath away. He caught her hands as she stepped to his side, and stood eye-to-eye with him.

He tucked her arm in his as they walked toward the front door. "Whatever the cost of your evening wear, it was well worth it. I have never seen you look so gorgeous."

Ruth's reply was an inadequate "Thank you." She had no idea how to react to such high praise. *Or was it flattery*?

Should she tell him she hadn't changed her original purchase? Why tempt fate? She would do well to get through this evening under the best of circumstances.

Ruth had visions of an eighteenth century ball with each couple being announced as they arrived. That was not the case. She and Henry slipped in unnoticed. They were scarcely through the door when Henry asked, "Shall we dance?"

The orchestra played *When You Were Sweet Sixteen*. Ruth placed her gloved hand into his palm. They swayed in perfect rhythm across the crowded dance floor. Being in Henry's arms felt so right. His smile did strange things to her pulse rate. She looked away and reveled in the magic of his nearness.

The dance was over much too soon.

Henry escorted Ruth toward the row of chairs that lined the back wall.

They were scarcely seated when other couples approached, none of whom Ruth recognized. Henry made introductions. Ruth tried in the beginning, to match names to faces. After a number of introductions, she decided it was a useless pursuit. Henry talked politely with the group gathered around. Ruth smiled and wished for the evening to be over.

The orchestra struck the first strains of *Alexander's Ragtime Band.* A young woman grabbed Henry's arm. "Dance with me, Mr. Jarrett."

Henry paled. "Miss Mansfield, I don't dance ragtime."

The young woman wasn't taking no for an answer. "I can teach you."

A middle-aged dowager-type woman, obviously the young woman's mama, scolded, "Lucinda, behave."

Lucinda wrinkled her nose at her mother before asking Ruth, "Mrs. Jarrett, do you mind if I dance with your husband?"

Ruth seethed with anger, or was it jealously? She hid her feelings behind a benevolent smile. "Mr. Jarrett doesn't need my permission."

Lucinda dragged Henry onto the dance floor. He looked over his shoulder at Ruth with a helpless expression on his face.

Ruth sat down. Henry Jarrett was too handsome for his own good. *Maybe I should have objected. Too late now.*

The crowd drifted away, except for the dapper young man who came to sit beside her. "My Lucinda has captured Mr. Jarrett away. Will you dance with me?"

Ruth shrugged and stood. Dancing was preferable to watching Henry dancing with Lucinda and executing a perfect Turkey Trot. She stepped into the young stranger's embrace. "I didn't catch your name."

The young man swung her onto the floor. "I am Edward Rutherford Covington the Third." He might have been announcing he was King George the Fifth. Ruth was out of breath when the dance was over. She was also provoked with Edward Rutherford Covington the Third. What pomposity, such arrogance.

Edward saw her to her chair, and wandered away, in search of Lucinda, no doubt.

The orchestra played *Memories.* From nowhere Dr. Mullins appeared to stand in front of her. "Ruth, you are the most beautiful woman at the ball. Will you dance with me?"

Ruth was set to refuse when Dr. Mullins added, "I don't usually dance at these affairs, but this was Letty's favorite song. She's been gone almost ten years, and I still miss her."

"I would be honored to dance with you." Ruth followed him onto the dance floor.

Dr. Mullins was a superb dancer, and a delightful partner. Ruth smiled down at him. "I apologize for my height. I'm wearing heels."

Dr. Mullins chuckled. "Stuff and nonsense. You look like a stately Aphrodite rising from the sea. My Letty was tall, six feet to be exact. I spied you the moment you walked in the door, rising above all these painted dolls."

"You saw me when Henry and I came in?" Ruth was so sure they had sneaked in unobserved. The idea that she could go unnoticed vanished.

Dr. Mullins stopped mid-way through the dance. "You and I must have a talk." He led her from the floor and back to the row of chairs along the wall. "Sit down."

Ruth sat.

Dr. Mullins sat beside her and took her hand in his. "Stop apologizing for your height. Celebrate it. Stop feeling sorry for yourself and treasure your God-given beauty." He squeezed her hand before letting go.

Henry came from the dance floor and sat on the other side of Ruth. "Good evening, Dr. Mullins. Count yourself lucky. You got in under the wire. The remainder of Ruth's dances are spoken for by none other than the lady's husband. That's me."

Dr. Mullins laughed. "If I were twenty years younger I would steal her from you." He walked away with his hands in his pockets, whistling *Memories.*

The remainder of the evening passed in a hazy glow of happiness. Ruth danced every dance with Henry. She felt like Cinderella. *May twelve o'clock never come.*

When the orchestra took a break, they went to the buffet table. Ruth was amazed at the array of food, some of which she had no idea what it was. She followed Henry's lead, choosing the dishes he chose. What if they tasted terrible? She didn't care. This was a magical night. She intended to enjoy every minute of it.

They found two chairs in a quiet corner, sat down, and balanced their plates on their laps.

Henry ate heartily. "Dancing makes an old man like me tired."

Ruth's contradiction came quickly. "You are not old, and you are the handsomest man at the ball." Heat crept into her cheeks. She turned her attention to her food, dismayed that such a statement came, unbidden, from her lips.

Henry smiled. "You, my dear, have made quite a fashion statement this evening. You make every other woman here look like an overdressed little girl."

Ruth's heart took flight. Her protective emotional barrier fell away. "Do you really think so?" *Stop it, you idiot. Vulnerable is the one thing you must never be.*

Henry sat his plate aside. "I most assuredly do. Shall we dance?"

Ruth stood and put her plate atop Henry's. "I would love to."

The orchestra played a popular new song, *Always Chasing Rainbows.*

Ruth slipped into her husband's arms and they glided across the floor. She fit so perfectly into his embrace.

A male tenor sang,

I'm always chasing rainbows
Watching clouds drifting by
My schemes are just like all my dreams
Ending in the sky

Some fellows look and find the sunshine
I always look and find the rain
Some fellows make a winning sometime
I never even make a gain, believe me

I'm always chasing rainbows
Waiting to find a little bluebird in vain

Reality replaced Ruth's rosy reverie. *Is that what I'm doing, searching in vain for what I can never hope to attain?* She smiled into her husband's eyes. Tomorrow she would slip back into her hum-drum routine. Tonight she would dream and pretend.

Chapter Eighteen

Cedar Gap, Texas
Saturday Evening
December 29th, 1917

Ruth sat in her chair in Henry's office. Henry occupied his usual place behind his desk. Their relationship had changed since the night of the Mayor's Ball. Maybe altered was a more apt word. She couldn't explain the nuances of differences, but they were there. Did Henry feel them too? He must, although he never mentioned the subject. Ruth held her peace and waited, with quiet anticipation, for further developments.

Henry asked, "Would you like to go out New Year's Eve?"

Ruth studied his face. She never tired of looking at him. He was the most distinguished man she knew, and the most brilliant. Behind that challenging façade was a man of gentle nature and modest dignity.

"Do you have a preference?" Henry put his elbows on his desk and set his chin in his hands.

His words pulled Ruth back to the present. "I would like to spend New Year's Eve at home with the children. We can pop popcorn in the fireplace. I will make hot chocolate, and we can play games. If you had rather go out--"

Henry dropped his arms and shook his head. "Staying home is an excellent idea. The children will love it."

They chatted amiably for the next fifteen minutes. As the clock on the wall neared nine-thirty, Ruth made preparations to go. There was one other thing she felt compelled to say. "There is only one Sunday left in 1917. The children are participating in a special program at the church the thirtieth."

The look on Henry's face said she should shut up. "Ruth, please, you know how I feel about attending church services."

"This is not a regular service. There will be no sermon. Joe and Jake will sing in the children's choir. Rosie is scheduled to read a portion of scripture."

Henry rubbed his hand over his eyes before pulling it across his face. "Sometimes I wonder about the wisdom of teaching children questionable truths."

Was this the man she had so recently dubbed as brilliant? "Are you saying I shouldn't take the children to church, or teach them from the Bible?"

Henry rose from his chair, walked to the window, and stood for several mind-bending minutes with his back to her and his hands clasped behind him.

Ruth was set to lambast him for his erudite ignorance. Her better judgment prevailed. She held her tongue.

Henry turned to face her. Indecision was written in every line in his face. He studied her expression for long moments before he spoke. "What would you say if the answer to that question was yes?"

Months ago Ruth made a vow to herself. She would not speak of Rachel to Henry, ever again. That vow was forgotten in the wake of her astonishment. "I would say Rachel would turn in her grave." *Don't say now what you will regret later.* That still small voice spoke in vain. "I promised Rachel on her death-bed I would bring up her children to be Christians. Don't deny me that right." She jumped to her feet. "You are an atheist."

A few long steps brought Henry to her side. "Calm down, Ruth. I am not an atheist. I am an agnostic. If it means that much to you, go ahead. Teach the children to be Christians."

Since Ruth came here from nursing school, she had shed buckets of tears. She was crying again. "Thank you. I'm sorry I lost my temper."

"This time you had reason. I shouldn't have provoked you." Henry gave her his handkerchief. "Dry your tears."

Ruth wiped her eyes and blew her nose before putting the handkerchief into her dress pocket. "Does this mean you won't go to church with us on Sunday?"

Henry put his hands on her shoulders and stared into her eyes. "Let's not have this argument again."

He was right about the futility of another argument. He wasn't right about being a Christian. Sooner or later she would make him see that. "Forgive me."

Henry brushed a stray strand of hair from Ruth's face. "There is nothing to forgive." He put his hands behind him and walked away, to stand once more by the window. "Good night, Ruth."

"Good night, Henry." She walked from the room with a half-dozen conflicting emotions churning around inside her.

*****

Cedar Gap, Texas
Monday Evening
December 31st, 1917

Ruth leaned back in an easy chair near the fireplace. The fire popped and crackled as it died to embers. Henry returned from tucking the children in bed, and sat in a matching chair across from her. "I did not know, until you came here, what a joy children can be. I am coming to see they are also a challenge. Next week I will begin reviewing applicants for a nursemaid. It shouldn't take long to find someone suitable."

Ruth was reluctant to argue with him after such a perfect evening, but he left her no alternative. "How will you know when you find someone suitable?"

Henry put his feet on the footstool in front of his chair. "I have hired, and fired, many people during my career. I know what makes a good employee."

Could Ruth make him understand without making his angry? She doubted it, but she had to try. She was aware that tact was not one of her strong points. She spoke slowly and chose her words carefully. "Hiring a nursemaid is not like hiring someone to work in your bank. Your employees work nine hours a day, and go home. Their skills are not the same as those required to tend to three small children five or six days out of every week."

Henry leaned his head on the chair back and stared at the ceiling. "Do you want to approve my choice?"

If his choice of a housekeeper was an indication of his choice for someone to tend his children, disaster lay ahead. "I want you and me to interview each applicant together. Then I want to see that applicant interact with the children."

Henry bolted upright in his chair. His feet hit the floor with a thud. "I don't have time to spend hours each day finding what you consider a proper nursemaid for three little children. I have a bank to run, and clients to confer with--" He stopped, mid-sentence, and ran his fingers through his hair. "Let's compromise. I will review all applicants and choose three or four acceptable candidates. We can interview those together."

"How will you go about finding applicants? Suppose I don't approve of any of your three or four candidates? What happens then? Do we begin the process all over again?"

Henry drummed his fingers on the arm of his chair. "I will put an ad in the *Cedar Gap Daily Clarion*. You can choose the best suited from those I select."

Ruth's patience was wearing thin. "What if after I observe each one interacting with the children, I don't like any of them?"

Henry shook his head and sighed. "Why can't you accept that I know best?"

His arrogance swept away Ruth's resolve to be tactful. "What makes you so sure you *do* know best?"

"Men are, by nature, more level-headed than women. Therefore, they are better equipped to make decisions." Henry leaned back and set his feet back on his foot stool. As if that statement settled the matter.

Ruth's voice dripped sarcasm. "What are your criteria, Mr. Superior

Decision-Maker, for a nursemaid for your children? Must she, or should I say he, be tall, short, fat, thin? Is twelve too young? Is ninety too old? Is being an atheist, excuse me, an agonistic, one requirement?"

Henry snapped, "You would argue with a fence post. I have never known a woman so opinionated, or so determined to have her way."

Ruth retorted, "How is it that you saying you know best reveals your superior, *level-headed* intelligence but me saying I know best makes me opinionated?"

Henry stood and extended his hands with his palms up. "The job is yours. *You* try finding a nursemaid. When you fail, I will come to your rescue. Good night, Ruth." So saying, he hurried from the room.

Ruth sat for a long time, staring into the dying fire. *I can't allow differences between Henry and me to taint the atmosphere of the children's home.*

She gazed into the smoking ashes and recalled how the constant tension that existed between her mama and papa made her childhood miserable. It was always there, just below the surface. She never knew when it would spark into a verbal free-for-all that resulted in hours, maybe days, of neither of them speaking to the other. She would do the only thing she could do, apologize, once again, to Henry.

Five minutes later, Ruth knocked on Henry's bedroom door.

"Who is it?"

Ruth replied, "It's me, Ruth. I must talk to you."

Henry opened the door. He was barefoot and shirtless. "Is there a problem?" He opened the door wider, and motioned for her to come inside.

Ruth entered.

Henry closed the door and stood against it.

The room was large, and decorated in muted shades of brown with touches of soft greens and bold yellows. The furniture was heavy and built for comfort. It was every inch, a man's room. *Did Rachel once share this room with Henry?*

Henry's voice impinged on her wandering thoughts. "Ruth, talk to me."

She turned to face him. "I came to apologize, again."

"I apologize also." He pointed to a chair. "Sit down."

Ruth sat, folded her hands in her lap, and stared down at them. "I said some ugly things to you. I didn't mean them."

Henry sat on the footstool in front of her, and took her hands in his, and looked into her eyes. "Accept my heartfelt request for forgiveness. I spoke before I thought."

A wealth of curly, dark hair grew on his chest. His hair was tousled. His nearness played havoc with Ruth's emotions. He smiled at her and her heart skipped a beat.

Henry rubbed the back of her hands with his thumbs. "We both behaved like children." The intimacy of the moment sent a thrill down her spine.

The softness of his voice was like a sweet caress. "I am sure you will find the right nursemaid for the children." He broke the spell between them by saying. "I always handled these matters for Rachel."

Ruth pulled her hands free, and jumped to her feet. "I have to go."

Henry walked her to the door. Before he opened it, he kissed her cheek. "Sleep well, Ruth." He held the door open for her.

"Good night, Henry." Ruth hurried down the hall, rubbing the spot Henry kissed. She ran up the stairs. She needed another perspective. "I will pen a letter to Flossie this very night."

Chapter Nineteen

Cedar Gap, Texas
Tuesday Afternoon
January 29th, 1918

Ruth put her elbows on her desk and dropped her head into her hands. She had lost count of the number of women she'd interviewed. Not one of them was right. One applicant remained. She knew before she interviewed her, that she wouldn't do. The woman was little more than a child herself. Ruth lifted her head.

The young woman stood just inside the front parlor doorway. "Am I next?" She was a tiny thing, and thin as a rail. Her dark hair was long and straight, her eyes big and green. She had on a dress that was two sizes too big, and too thin to be worn in the dead of winter. She looked as if, at any moment, she might bolt and run.

Ruth motioned for her to come in and sit down. "What is your name?"

The young woman kept looking over her shoulder. She came into the room, but remained standing. "My name is Faith."

"Do you have a last name?"

"Just Faith."

Ruth looked up from the application before her. She was tired and distraught. "You may go."

Tears coursed down the young woman's pale face. "Please don't send me away. I love children. I will be the best nursemaid you can imagine. Give me a chance to prove myself."

The poor little thing shook like a leaf. Was she cold or scared? Maybe a little of both. Pity replaced Ruth's agitation. "Would you like me to take you home?"

Faith caught one of her shaking hands in the other. "I don't have a home, and I can't go back where I came from."

This waif was frightened out of her wits. *I will soon get to the bottom of this.* "You obviously have a problem. Maybe I can help you solve it." She stood and walked in the woman's direction.

Faith shook her head and said, with doomsday finality. "No one can solve my problem."

Ruth led her to the sofa. "Nothing can be so bad that it doesn't have a solution." She pushed the shaking creature down onto a cushion, and sat beside her. "Tell me what is troubling you." Ruth's curiosity mixed with her pity. It was a compelling combination.

The young woman dropped her head and stared at the floor. "I don't dare tell anyone."

"I'll make a deal with you," Ruth said. "The three children I need a nursemaid for will be home from school at any moment. You can show me your nursemaid skills. If I think you are the right person for the job, it's yours, but only if you tell me about your past. Is it a deal?"

Faith looked up as her face radiated with a beautiful smile. "Yes, Ma'am. Thank you, Mrs. Jarrett, so much."

The children came bursting through the front door, first Jake, then Joe. Rosie brought up the rear.

Ruth called, "Hang your coats in the foyer closet and come into the front parlor."

The trio responded with a chorus of "Yes, Ma'am."

Jake was the first to charge into the parlor. "Hey, you know what? It may snow tomorrow. If it does--" He halted, and pointed his finger at the stranger on the couch. "Who is she?"

Joe was close behind him. "Hi, Aunt Mama."

Rosie stepped into the room. She stood behind her brothers. "Mind your manners, boys. Hi, Aunt Mama."

Ruth motioned for the children to come nearer. She hugged and greeted each child before introducing Faith as a prospective nursemaid.

The corners of Jake's mouth turned down as he questioned, on an intake of breath, "Another one?"

Joe extended his hand. "I am very glad to meet you, Miss Faith."

Rosie stepped from behind Joe. "Is your name really Faith?"

To Faith's credit, she neither made light of the question, nor did she scold, saying something like the question was personal, or children shouldn't ask such questions of adults. She said, in forthright tones, "Yes, it is. Why do you ask?"

Rosie moved nearer. "My name is really Pearl Rose, but my friends call me Rosie."

So many of the women Ruth interviewed spoke to the children in condescending tones. Not Faith. She smiled and said, "Rosie is a nice name."

"You can call me Rosie, if you would like."

"I would like that very much," Faith replied.

Rosie was not usually friendly with strangers. The boys responded well too. "Go now, children. Mrs. Murphy has hot chocolate and cookies for you. I will be in later to help you with your homework."

In unison, the twins shouted, "Bye, Miss Faith," and rushed toward the kitchen.

Rosie curtsied. "Bye, Miss Faith. I hope to see you again." She followed the twins toward the kitchen.

Faith leaned forward. "Did I do okay?"

She may not be perfect, but she is the best I'm going to find. "The job is yours, but only after I learn more about your background. It's getting late, and Mr. Jarrett will be home soon. Come back tomorrow morning and we will settle the details." As an afterthought, she added, "Button your coat and wear your cap. It is late and freezing cold outside."

Terror leaped into Faith's eyes. "I don't have a coat, and if I go back where I came from, I will have to stay."

Was she telling the truth? If the look of terror in her eyes was any indication, she was. Ruth couldn't send this poor creature out in the cold with no coat, and no place to go. "You can stay here tonight. If things work out, this will be your permanent home. If not..." Her voice trailed away on the end of a sigh.

Faith folded her hands beneath her chin and bowed her head. "Thank you, Heavenly Father, for taking care of me."

Ruth was caught unawares. "Are you a Christian?"

Faith scooted to the end of the sofa and huddled there. "Yes, Ma'am, I am. If you object to that, I will go."

"I don't object," Ruth hurried to assure her. "I am pleased. I, too, am a Christian." *Even though I don't always act like one.* "Come with me to the kitchen, I will introduce you to my housekeeper and cook, Mrs. Murphy." No doubt, Mrs. Murphy would object to another domestic in the house.

To Ruth's total surprise, Mrs. Murphy welcomed Faith with open arms. "Gracious child, you must be freezing in that thin dress. I have an extra sweater in my room. Come and I'll show you the way to our quarters. You have a private bedroom. We will share a bathroom."

Ruth stood staring as the two women disappeared down the hall toward the back of the house. Jake calling to her pulled her attention back to the children. "Aunt Mama, I need help with my arithmetic."

Ruth sat beside Jake. "What is your problem?"

Jake tapped his pencil on the open book before him. "*This* problem is my problem. I don't know how to do it."

When homework was completed, Jake and Joe went to the back parlor to play. Rosie curled up in a chair in the front parlor to read her book.

Mrs. Murphy returned with Faith who wore a sweater that swallowed her. Mrs. Murphy made dinner. Faith insisted on helping. Ruth went to her room to write Flossie a long letter.

She was sealing the envelope when a knock sounded on her door. Ruth called out, "Come in. It's not locked."

The door opened and Henry entered.

"Good evening. I am glad to see you have some time for yourself. I met the new nursemaid."

Ruth pointed to a chair. "What do you think of her?"

Henry eased into the chair. "At first sight, I thought she was too young for the job. Then I saw her with the children. They get along well together. She and Mrs. Murphy have hit it off well, too. That's a plus."

The knot of tension in Ruth's stomach untied. "Do you approve?"

"I do indeed." Henry stood and offered her his arm. "I came to escort you down to dinner."

Ruth put her hand through his arm. They descended the stairs and walked down the hall toward the dining room.

Chapter Twenty

Cedar Gap, Texas
Wednesday Afternoon
January 30th, 1918

Ruth borrowed, without asking permission, Henry's office. It was the only private room in the house. She sat behind Henry's desk waiting for Faith to appear. The conversation between her and Faith couldn't be heard outside these four walls.

The morning had gone well. Faith walked the children to school and returned to sit in the kitchen with Mrs. Murphy.

Miraculously Mrs. Murphy found a coat, a few dresses, even a decent pair of shoes for Faith to wear. Ruth didn't know where they came from. She suspected they were things Rachel had long ago tossed in the rag bag. She didn't ask. It was enough that Mrs. Murphy had taken Faith under her wing.

Ruth spent the remainder of the morning going over the children's schedule with Faith. Her new nursemaid was a quick study, and anxious to please.

Footsteps sounding down the hall alerted Ruth to the approach of her newest employee. After one rap, she called, "Come in."

Faith entered and closed the door behind her before sitting down in the chair Ruth usually occupied. "Thank you for the clothes, Mrs. Jarrett." Perspiration stood on her top lip. Her voice quivered.

"You are welcome." Ruth extended one hand. "You don't have to be afraid of me. I'm not going to hurt you, but I can't let you continue as the children's nursemaid until you tell me something about yourself."

"Where do I begin?"

"Begin with where you came from and why you can't go back."

Faith gripped the arms of her chair and took a deep breath before blurting out in one hasty sentence, "I came from Miss Lola's Fun House across the tracks."

Ruth's breath caught in her throat. "That's a -- house of ill repute."

"I know." Faith hung her head.

"Whatever were you doing in a place like that?" *That is a stupid question.* "Don't answer that."

Tears rolled down Faith's cheeks. "I met Miss Lola just after Papa kicked me out because I was going to have a baby and I wasn't married. Miss Lola promised if I would work for her in the kitchen, until the baby came, she would give me room and board. She said her good deed was with the understanding that after my baby was born, I would become one of her 'girls'." Faith choked on a sob.

Ruth was incensed. "Good deed, my Aunt Fanny. The woman should be horse whipped." She hated being so persistent, but if she was to entrust the children to this woman's care, she needed to know more.

Faith wiped tears from her eyes and snubbed before rubbing her nose on the sleeve of her dress. "I was going to run away after I had my baby."

Ruth hated being the devil's advocate, but she pressed on. "What made you decide to stay?"

"I saw what Miss Lola did to girls who tried to get away from that horrible place. I was too scared to try to run away. What if Smokey Joe hurt Hope? Then Hope died, and I didn't care anymore." Faith lifted her head. "Hope was what I named my little girl."

Ruth came around Henry's desk, pulled Faith to her feet, and put a comforting arm around her shoulder. "Who is Smokey Joe?" She led Faith toward the couch against the wall.

"Smokey Joe works for Miss Lola. She calls him and his two friends her porters. They keep order in Miss Lola's house. They also chase down and bring back girls who run away. They do terrible things to those girls they catch. I've seen some of them when Smokey Joe brought them back. Those men beat them and do other awful things to them."

A chill of fear ran down Ruth's spine. It was accompanied by a fiery blaze of anger. She sat on Henry's leather couch and patted the space beside her. "Sit down and tell me more. Who is the father of your baby?" Faith would not bring such shame on herself by telling this story if they were not true. *Poor child, small wonder she's afraid of everything and everybody.*

Faith sat on the edge of the couch. "I can't tell you that. I can never tell anyone that. If I do, that man will do terrible things to Papa and Mama."

So many things fell into place. "He forced you, didn't he?"

Faith buried her face in her hands and wept. "Yes."

Ruth pulled Faith's hands from her face and held them in a tight grasp. "You must tell. This man should be punished for what he did to you."

"I did tell someone, my papa. He didn't believe me. If my own papa didn't believe me, why should anyone else?"

Ruth assured her, "I believe you." In a sterner voice, she demanded, "What is this man's name?"

Faith pulled her hands from Ruth's grasp and doubled them into fists. She shook so her teeth knocked together. "Please don't make me tell. If I do he will say it isn't true. No one would take my word over his, and he could do terrible things to Mama and Papa."

Ruth stopped her badgering. That didn't stop her determination to eventually find out who this man was, and see that he was punished for what he did to this pathetic woman-child. "We will drop the subject for now. Consider yourself hired as of yesterday."

Faith unclenched her fists and folded her hands beneath her chin. "Will you pray with me, Mrs. Jarrett?" She bowed her head.

Ruth prayed at Ladies' Bible Study meetings. On occasion, she prayed at the beginning of her Sunday School Class. Those weren't real prayers. They were empty words spoken to impress others. *I am ashamed.* "Heavenly Father," she began. Those words sank deep into her heart. A living, loving God *was* her Father. He was also Faith's Father. He would not turn His back on her as her earthly father had. "Thank you for sending us Faith." She choked on her own words. "Amen."

Faith prayed a short, simple prayer of thanksgiving before breathing amen. She dropped her hands and raised her head. "Thank you, Mrs. Jarrett."

Ruth reined in her emotions. "Go now. And get an after school snack ready for your charges."

Long after Faith vanished down the hall, Ruth sat and worked at setting her thoughts in order. What would Henry say about Faith's questionable background? Nothing if he didn't know. She *would* tell him, but not for a while. *Isn't silence one form of lying?* It was, and she knew it. Ruth left the office and locked the door behind her. *I will tell him when he asks.*

*****

January passed in a bluster of cold and chilling winds.

February rode in on a blustery norther. Faith took over much of the care of the children. Ruth was free to lead a more active social life. The second Wednesday of each month was meeting day for the church's Ladies Auxiliary. Ruth volunteered to host the meeting in February. The second Wednesday fell on February the thirteenth. One day before Valentine's Day. She would decorate the parlor using red crepe paper streamers and white crepe paper and red hearts.

Ruth approached Mrs. Murphy with caution, sure she would complain about extra work. She came into the kitchen to find Faith and Mrs. Murphy sitting at the table, pouring over Mrs. Murphy's large collection of recipes.

Ruth sat in a chair across from Mrs. Murphy. "I will be hosting the Ladies Auxiliary tomorrow. I expect about fifteen ladies. I would like three dozen cookies to serve. If possible I would like them to be heart-shaped and colored red."

Faith touched Mrs. Murphy's arm. "May I help? I would love to learn how to make cookies. *Can* you make them red and heart-shaped?"

Mrs. Murphy's face shaped into the semblance of a smile. "Of course

I can. All I need besides a batch of sugar cookie doughred food coloring, is a heart-shaped cookie cutter."

Ruth's jaw dropped. This was a Mrs. Murphy she didn't know. "I am also going to decorate the front parlor with red and white crepe paper. Would either of you like to help?"

Faith answered for the two of them. "We would. Mrs. Murphy knows all about making a room beautiful. You should see the pillows and dresser scarves she put in my room."

Maybe a part of my inability to get along with Mrs. Murphy lies with me. "Mrs. Murphy is talented in many ways," Ruth said. She added, "Her cooking is superb."

Faith nodded. "I know. She is teaching me how to make Parker House rolls."

Mrs. Murphy stood and closed the lid on the wooden box holding her recipes. "I do my best. It's time to start dinner."

Faith pushed back her chair. "And time for me to fetch the children home." As she and Ruth walked toward the foyer, she asked, "Isn't Mrs. Murphy the sweetest lady?"

What a difference perspective makes. "She seems to be very fond of you."

Faith opened the foyer closet door and reached for her coat. "She and I talk every night. I told her all about what happened to me after -- after that man attacked me. She was nice to me too, just like you were." She slipped her arms into her coat. "God led me to you and Mrs. Murphy. I thank Him every day and every night that He did."

If Mrs. Murphy knew of Faith's background, Ruth had no doubt that Henry would soon be privy to the same information. She went into the living room and sat on the sofa. She would tell Henry tonight when they talked. *As if I had a choice.*

Chapter Twenty-One

Cedar Gap, Texas
Monday Evening
February 12th, 1918

Ruth looked forward, as always, to the time she spent with Henry each evening. She came into the room, sat in her chair and smiled at the handsome man who sat behind his desk. "Good evening, Henry."

Henry returned her smile. "Good evening, Ruth." He opened the top drawer of his desk and took out a small satin box. "This is for you. It's a small token of my affection." He offered her the box. "Happy Valentine's Day."

A muffled sound caught in Ruth's throat. She paled, searching for words to express her gratitude. "I-I don't know what to say."

"Open it."

Ruth obeyed. Nestled inside was a beautiful cameo broach. "It's lovely." She pinned it to the neck of her dress. "Thank you. I am entertaining the Ladies Church Auxiliary tomorrow afternoon. I will wear this with such pride. I didn't buy you a gift. I should have."

"No problem." Henry waved his hand in a dismissive gesture. "You are entertaining church friends? I am glad. Perhaps you will also have time now to enjoy some of your hobbies, whatever they may be. Rachel wrote poetry. Some of it was quite exquisite."

Those words stung. Why would he mention Rachel? Was he comparing the two of them? If that was the case, Ruth was sure to fall short. "I am not Rachel."

"Did I offend you?" Henry asked, with a surprised note in his voice. "If I did, forgive me. That was not my intent."

Ruth repented of her hasty words. "I know that. Thank you for the broach, and for approving my choice of a nursemaid for the children." *I must tell him about Faith's past, and the sooner, the better.* "There are some things about Faith you should know."

"She seems to get on well with Mrs. Murphy." Henry raised an eyebrow. "I thought you were happy with her work."

Ruth resolved to ease into the subject. "I am pleased with her work. She and Mrs. Murphy have become fast friends."

Henry straightened in his chair. "For heaven's sake, Ruth, tell me what is bothering you."

Ruth's resolve to be tactful retreated, to be replaced by a flare of temper. "Before Faith came to work here she was at Miss Lola's Fun

House."

Henry jumped to his feet. "Good heavens, Ruth, Miss Lola's Fun House is--"

"I know what Miss Lola's house is." Ruth stood and grasped the sides of his desk. "Sit down and shut up. Let me tell you the complete story. Then you can rant at me."

To her total amazement, Henry sat and remained silent as Ruth related, in disorderly sentences, the story Faith told her. She completed her explanation, stopped, and waited for Henry to voice his disapproval.

He shook his head from side to side. "You never cease to amaze me. On the outside you are opinionated and abrupt. On the inside, you are soft as silk. What do you want me to say?"

Ruth sat down in her chair. This was not the reaction she expected. "Can she stay?"

Henry rubbed his chin with his thumb and forefinger as he looked at her with a strange glint in his eyes. "If I said 'send her away,' would you?"

Ruth stood once more. "Don't play games with me. I want a straight answer, and I want it now."

Henry barked, "Sit down."

Ruth obeyed, even though it took every ounce of her self-restraint to do so.

Henry stood, pushed his chair back with his foot, and walked to the windows. With both hands behind him, and his feet spread apart, he stared at her. "Under the circumstances, I see no alternative. She can stay, but remember, we have a position to maintain in Cedar Gap. I don't want trouble. Promise me you won't try to find the man who attacked Faith."

Ruth lifted her right hand. "I promise." She should have been glad, but her heart was heavy. Henry gave her a Valentine Day's gift, and set the scene for a romantic visit. She destroyed it all. Only after the fact did she realize what a mistake she had made. "Thank you for the lovely cameo. It's beautiful, and I love it."

Henry retraced his footsteps, and sat again, in his chair. "You are welcome. Good night, Ruth."

He was sending her away, dismissing her as if her presence offended him. *Maybe it does.* "Good night, Henry. Sleep well."

*****

Cedar Gap, Texas
Tuesday Afternoon
February 13th, 1918

The front parlor was festively decorated. Faith hung the last red construction paper heart, completing the row of hearts that adorned the white crepe ribbon circling the wall near the ceiling. She stepped down from her chair. Moving back, she viewed her handiwork. "They look beautiful. I knew they would. Your guests will be surprised."

Ruth put scissors and pieces of red construction paper into a bag. "The cold weather and the wind may limit my number of guests." The words were hardly out of her mouth when a rap sounded on the front door. She hurried to answer. "Take the bag to the kitchen, and help Mrs. Murphy prepare the tea cart."

"Yes, Ma'am." Faith hurried toward the kitchen.

Ruth opened the front door

Arabella Higgins stood on the front porch. She clutched her Bible in one hand, and held her purse in the other. "Gracious, the weather is terrible." She stepped inside. She was a tall angular middle-aged woman with an autocratic face and an arrogant air. "Sister Trigg will not be here today. She has that three-day-fever that's going around. I have prepared a lesson for today's meeting."

Mrs. Trigg had sent no such message to Ruth. "Was this at Mrs. Trigg's request?"

Arabella laid her and Bible and purse on a chair and was in the process of removing her coat. "When I learned the poor soul was ill, I called and informed her of my intent to take charge." She hung her coat on a wall peg.

Before Ruth could answer, three other guests appeared on her porch. Before she could usher them inside, two more ladies arrived. Edna McCarthy was the last one inside. "None of the other members will be here," she said, as she removed her coat. "They either have the three-day fever, or they are caring for family members who do."

The group entered the front parlor, sat down, and expressed admiration for Ruth's lovely decorations.

Before Ruth could answer, Arabella took command, an action Ruth found both ill-mannered and offensive. "Sister Trigg is ill," Arabella said. "I will be bringing today's lesson. Open your Bibles to the Gospel of John, Chapter One."

Ruth looked at Edna who sat beside her. Edna whispered in her ear, "Pay no attention to Arabella. She a trifle domineering."

Arabella Higgins was a tyrant. She might dictate to the other members of the auxiliary, but not to Ruth. "One moment please, Arabella."

Arabella paused and lowered her Bible. "I beg your pardon."

"Since Sister Trigg appointed no one in particular to bring a lesson, and the meeting is in my home, I have decided we will each give our personal testimony. Then we will have a prayer session."

A collective intake of breath waited for Arabella's reply. When it came, it hit Ruth like a slap in the face. "I find it offensive that you have decorated your home to honor a pagan god." She waved her hand in an all-encompassing circle. "Cupid indeed."

Ruth should be angry. She wasn't. She did feel pity for this overbearing, dictatorial woman. "Do you see any cupids here? Of course you don't, and you won't. The red represents the blood of Christ that He shed for us. The white is illustrative of God's purity. The hearts speak of Christ's love for His children."

Faith appeared in the doorway, pushing a teacart. "Mrs. Murphy said I should bring this in." She stopped the cart before Ruth and turned to go.

She was midway across the floor when Arabella shouted, "Stop where you are, young woman!"

Faith stopped and turned to face Arabella. A look of sheer terror spread across her face.

Arabella's eyes narrowed as she cast a dagger-like stare in Ruth's direction. "Do you know who this young woman is?"

Ruth went back to her chair. "I do." She sat and met Arabella's heated gaze.

"You dare let trash like this serve good Christian women?" Arabella pointed a condemning finger in Faith's direction.

Faith headed for the door.

"Come back," Ruth called, "and stand where you were."

Faith's alarmed expression said she had rather not, but she did.

Ruth lifted the tray of cookies from the tea cart, and came to stand directly in front of Arabella. "In lieu of stones, I offer you cookies. Be my guest, cast the first cookie."

A titter of giggles echoed through the room.

Arabella Higgins looked as though she might explode. "I have never been so insulted before in my life." She grabbed her Bible and her purse, and sped from the room, saying as she fled, "Our pastor shall hear of your atrocious behavior."

"May I go now?" Faith asked.

Ruth nodded her consent.

Over the slam of the front door, the remaining women gathered around Ruth.

Edna put her arm around Ruth's shoulders. "Don't pay any heed to Arabella's threats. She reports someone to Pastor Cooper at least once a week"

I have made some friends, but I fear I have also made one bad enemy. Ruth asked, "Shall we continue with our session?" With one accord, the others agreed to carry on with the meeting.

Chapter Twenty-Two

Cedar Gap, Texas
Tuesday Evening
February 26th, 1918

Ruth came into Henry's office and greeted him with her usual, "Good evening, Henry."

Henry's solemn expression was not a harbinger of good news. "Good evening, my dear. Please sit down. We have something important to discuss."

Ruth eased onto the edge of her chair. Henry had called her dear. He did that more and more often these days. Ruth tried not to attach too much importance to it, yet she felt a glow of pleasure each time he did. "Is this bad news?"

"That," Henry replied, "depends on your point of view."

Ruth's clash with Arabella Higgins did much to bring her to the realization that she must control her temper. Having Faith in the house had a settling effect on her, and helped her to better understand Mrs. Murphy. Once she remarked to Faith, "Dear girl, you have the patience of a saint."

Faith replied, "I am a saint. We all are if we have Jesus as our savior." Ruth took those words to heart, and worked, from that day, to mend her ways.

Words that would have set her temper flaring six months ago now made her smile. "What, pray, is *your* point of view on this unknown subject?"

Henry returned her smile. "The subject is Mrs. Murphy. She and I have talked. I advised her to sell her little house and the few acres it sits on. She only stays there on weekends. It's in sad need of repairs. She lacks the funds to have them done. I can invest the money she gets from its sale, thus assuring her a small income for the remainder of her life."

Ruth raised a questioning eyebrow. "Where would she live?"

"She will move in with us permanently, but only if you agree."

Ruth was astounded by his request. She and Mrs. Murphy seldom disagreed anymore, still--

Henry asked, with some uncertainty, "Maybe if you could think of Mrs. Murphy as something more than a servant--"

The hesitant look in his eyes pained Ruth. Was she that much of a tyrant? Hasty hindsight made her realize, at times, she was. "You are a good man, Henry Jarrett. You have my approval."

Henry came around his desk, pulled Ruth to her feet, took her in his arms and kissed her. This time it was not a peck on her cheek. It was a gentle, deep kiss on her lips. He raised his head. "You, my dear, are a fine, caring woman, even though you do everything in your power to keep others from learning your secret."

Ruth's breath came in little gasps. She could stay here in his arms forever.

Henry released her, and stepped back. "Would you like to be the one to tell Mrs. Murphy the news?"

Ruth touched her lips with her fingertips. "I -- yes."

"Are you all right?"

Ruth was better than all right. She was elated. "We will all tell her, the twins, Rosie, Faith, and me. It will be a party. Would you like to come?"

Henry returned to sit behind his desk. "I think not, but a party is a grand idea. Good night, my dear."

"Good night, Henry."

*****

Cedar Gap, Texas
Saturday Evening
March 2nd, 1918

Jake sat on a bench at the kitchen table and sang, "We're going to have a party. We're going to have a party. We're going--"

Joe came from behind and clamped one hand over his twin's mouth. "Be quiet, dummy."

Jake shook himself free. "I'm not a dummy, you are."

Joe sat beside his brother. "I am not."

"Are too."

Ruth put glasses and a pitcher of punch on the table. "Stop it, both of you."

Rosie came down the stairs with a large sack holding five wrapped packages. "Where shall I put Mrs. Murphy's presents?"

Ruth moved toward the Hoosier. "Put them on the end of the table."

As Rosie took a seat between Jake and Joe, Jake leaned around her to ask his twin, "What did you get Mrs. Murphy?"

Joe opened his mouth to speak.

Rosie cuffed Joe on his arm. "Aunt Mama says we're not supposed to tell." She shook her finger in Jake's face and gave him a disdainful look. "You had better behave."

Jake stuck out his tongue at Rosie.

She ignored him and asked Ruth, "Where is Mrs. Murphy?"

Ruth arranged cookies on a plate. "She and Faith went to visit Clara and her little boys." Ruth sent them with the made-up excuse of taking Clara two loaves of Mrs. Murphy's yeast bread.

Mrs. Murphy balked at going. "I made the bread. Why should you expect me to deliver it too?"

Faith insisted. "Please come with me. It's a nice day outside. We can visit as we walk. I won't be scared if you're with me." She stood behind Mrs. Murphy and winked at Ruth.

Reluctantly, and complaining, Mrs. Murphy agreed to go.

Faith and Mrs. Murphy entered the kitchen as Ruth put the finishing touches on her table decorations. "Welcome to your party, Mrs. Murphy."

Mrs. Murphy frowned in Faith's direction. "What is going on here?"

Faith threw her arms around Mrs. Murphy's neck. "I'm so happy. Mrs. Jarrett says she wants you to live here all the time. Please say you will."

The children joined in with "Please, Mrs. Murphy," and "Say you will, Mrs. Murphy."

Jake added, "We each bought a present for you to celebrate."

Ruth shushed the children before saying, "We are all hoping you will say yes."

Tears gathered in Mrs. Murphy's eyes. "I did speak to Mr. Jarrett about selling my house." She wiped at her eyes with the edge of her apron. "Are you sure?"

Ruth's answer rang out across the room. "We are all very sure."

Faith led Mrs. Murphy to a chair. "Sit here."

Mrs. Murphy crying? Ruth thought her incapable of shedding tears. Moisture collected in her own eyes. How wrong she had been about so many things. "Open your presents, Mrs. Murphy, and we will all have punch and cookies, and celebrate."

Mrs. Murphy was as excited as a child. "Which one shall I open first?"

Faith pulled a chair near and sat beside Mrs. Murphy. "It doesn't matter, but please open one. I'm so excited to know what's inside."

"I'll start with the largest." Mrs. Murphy reached for a brightly wrapped box. She opened it, folding the wrapping paper as she carefully removed each piece. "I can save this to use again. Waste not, want not, I always say."

The gift was from Ruth. It was a warm winter coat, to replace the worn one Mrs. Murphy had now.

Mrs. Murphy gasped in surprise. "I -- Thank you so much, Mrs. Jarrett."

Ruth batted her eyes to clear her vision. "You are welcome, and the name is Ruth."

Mrs. Murphy hugged the coat to her chest. "Thank you, Ruth."

Jake said, "Open another one."

Mrs. Murphy reached for the biggest of the four remaining packages.

Rosie shouted, "That's mine." Her voice lowered. "I know you will like it. Papa told me what to choose."

Mrs. Murphy opened the package and drew a heavy breath. "Oh, my." Inside the box were a dozen skeins of soft blue wool yarn and four pairs of knitting needles of various sizes. "Thank you, Rosie. I do like it, very much."

Mrs. Murphy reached for the next box. "This is from Jake. Thank you, Jake." Inside the oblong box were several yards of blue checked gingham, spools of thread, a packet of needles, a pair of scissors, and a thimble.

Jake asked, "Do you like it? Papa said you didn't have a blue gingham dress and there is enough material in there to make one."

Henry had a hand in what the children bought. *He's a dear sweet man, and I like him -- very much.*

Mrs. Murphy opened the package from Joe. It contained two long flannel granny night gowns, and a warm, fleecy robe. "Joe, they are beautiful, and just what I need."

Joe grinned. "Papa helped me too."

Mrs. Murphy opened the last package.

"That one is from me," Faith said, with a touch of pride.

Mrs. Murphy smiled as she untied the string around the gift. Inside was a hand knitted cap and scarf. Mrs. Murphy breathed, "You made these for me?"

Faith was all smiles. "I did, and I loved doing it." She threw her arms around Mrs. Murphy's neck. "I love you, Mrs. Murphy."

Mrs. Murphy blushed. "Such carryings on." She pushed her chair back, and stood. "I thank you all very much for making me feel I belong here." She gathered he packages together. "Let me put my gifts away and we will have cookies and punch."

Chapter Twenty-Three

Cedar Gap, Texas
Wednesday Evening
March 27th, 1918

Ruth knocked on Henry's office door. How much she looked forward to her evening visits with him. Over the past months, she had come to see Henry Jarrett in a different light. He was no longer the man who held a tight rein on her through her obstinate teenage years. He was a gentle, thoughtful, kind, and very handsome male. He was also her husband, but in name only. Would he ever want it any other way? She was beginning to wonder.

He opened the door. His expression was set in angry lines. "Come in, my dear."

He was doing it again, sending her mixed signals. If she had learned anything over the past few months, it was to think before she made some tactless remark. She remained silent as she came into the room and sat in her chair. Once seated, she asked, "How are you this evening, Henry?"

"Very well. Thank you." He sat in the chair behind his desk. "Has all been going well?" His tone was cold enough to send chills down her spine. She wrapped her arms around her middle and shivered.

How well she could read his moods. Something had upset him. Which was worse, confronting him, and getting everything out into the open, or playing this cat-and-mouse game of what-is-troubling-you-now? Ruth should give him credit where credit was due. "You were right about Mrs. Murphy. Since our welcome here party for her, she is a different person. I never thought I would grow to like her, but I have."

Henry turned his head to one side. His expression remained frozen in place. "That's good."

Ruth refused to play games any longer. "What's good, that you were right, or that I have learned to like Mrs. Murphy?"

"Both," Henry replied. "The knowledge that you approve of something I said or did *and* that you like Mrs. Murphy eases my fear that you might someday decide this is all too much for you and leave."

Ruth was appalled. "I would never leave you, or the children."

Henry's icy expression melted into lines of doubt. "Do you stay out of some sense of duty?"

Ruth sat up and squared her shoulders. "No. I stay because -- no."

"Tell me, Ruth, why do you stay?"

Why did she feel so defenseless? "I love the children and you are my husband."

"That hardly seems reason enough for a lifetime commitment from one as young as you. Suppose some dashing young blade comes along, someone nearer your age, and offers you his love and a life free from the responsibilities of a ready-made family? What happens then?" He sat, waiting for her response.

She had to disabuse him of this absurd idea. Ruth spoke her heart. "I love the children too much to ever think of leaving them." Swift realization made her recognize a truth that, for the past few months, she refused to admit, even to herself. "Whatever would I do with a 'dashing young blade'? I prefer older men, those with some maturity and common sense, like my husband."

Henry gasped as the tense lines in his face relaxed. "Do you know what you just said?"

"I do, and I meant every word of it." If he rejected her now, she would at least know where she stood with him.

"For the last few months, I have been so afraid you would leave me before I could show you how much I have learned to care for you. I can bear it no longer. I must know what your feelings are for me."

"You care for me?" Ruth asked in amazement.

"I love you and I admire you." Henry folded his hands atop his desk. "I don't know when it happened, but it did. Over the last few months, I have been so afraid of losing you."

Ruth asked, on a tremulous breath, "Do you think there is a chance we could--?"

Henry hastened to say, "I think there is every chance, but first we must talk about several things, beginning with Rachel."

Ruth shook her head in protest. "It's not necessary."

"It is," Henry answered. "This one time, then never again."

Ruth grasped the arms of her chair, dreading what she was to hear, but knowing it must be said. "Speak."

Henry closed his eyes and lifted his head to stare at the ceiling. "I loved Rachel from the first moment I saw her."

Ruth cringed. This was not what she wanted to hear. It was what she expected. "Go on."

Henry dropped his head, opened his eyes, and stared at her. "I found her one night working late in her teller's cage at the bank. She couldn't balance her accounts. I helped her find her mistake then took her to dinner. She asked me if I was going to fire her. Can you imagine?"

Ruth could, and she said so. "Rachel had good reason to be afraid of men. Papa saw to that. He often came home drunk. Rachel and I always hid in our bedroom closet. Rachel was so scared her teeth would knock together. I was afraid too, but not in the way Rachel was. I wanted to hit Papa with a baseball bat. Rachel always stopped me from trying. She said I would get hurt because my papa was a big man and I was a little girl."

Henry swallowed. "I didn't know it was that bad. Rachel never spoke of her childhood. The two of you grew up in the same home, under the same circumstances. It made Rachel afraid of her shadow. It made you always come out swinging. I understand some things now that I questioned many times before."

Ruth's eyes glazed with tears. "Talking about our childhood always caused us grief. For me, it still does."

"We will say no more about that time in your life." Henry cleared his throat. "Rachel never disputed any decision I made. She was, in many ways, as much a child as Rosie is now. We were happy together. When I learned she had cancer, it broke my heart."

"I should have been here to care for her." Ruth brushed at a tear.

"I should have told you sooner," Henry said. "I wanted to, but Rachel begged me not to. She wanted you to graduate nursing school. She knew how important it was to you. When she first asked me to promise I'd marry you after she was gone, I thought she had taken leave of her senses. The more I pondered over the idea, the more sensible it seemed. I knew how much you cared for the children. I thought I would never love again. If you agreed, why not? When you did agree, I was surprised. Why did you?"

Ruth spoke slowly, and truthfully. "I was afraid if I didn't, you would marry someone else, someone who might mistreat the children."

Henry gave an indignant snort. "I would never let anyone mistreat my children."

A lump rose in Ruth's throat. "I know that now. I didn't know it then. I was afraid too that they might learn to love her more than they loved me." She twisted her hands together. "I have come to admire and respect you very much."

Henry smiled. "Admiration and respect are a start. If you are willing to try, we can begin to build our relationship into something solid and lasting."

Ruth was more than willing. "I would like that. You must show me the way. I don't know where to start."

His smile sent her pulses racing. "You always challenge me. That is one of the things I have come to love about you, that and your strength. I have a wife who stands beside me. We will meet the trials life throws at us shoulder-to-shoulder, and together, conquer them. Now, this moment, tonight, is the beginning of our new life together." He came around his desk, pulled her to her feet, and took her in his arms.

His embrace was warm. Ruth put her arms around his neck, and stared up into his eyes. "There is one other thing I must say."

Henry stepped back. "Yes?"

"You once told me any woman who came to you must come because of her need, not yours." She closed the short distance between them and laid her head on his shoulder. "I come to you now because I need you, I always will."

Henry swung her around in his arms. "That need is mutual, I assure you." He set her down and kissed her as she had never been kissed before.

When she could breathe, Ruth said, "Make me your wife, Henry, your real wife."

"I have waited so long to hear those words."

Arm-in-arm, they walked out of the office, down the hall to Henry's bedroom. Henry led her inside and closed the door.

Chapter Twenty-Four

Cedar Gap, Texas
Wednesday Morning
April 24th, 1918

Mrs. Murphy straightened from raking around tomato plants and put her hand to her back. "The garden is going to make a bumper crop this year. It will make it easier to get through those meatless Tuesdays and wheatless Wednesdays that lie ahead."

Faith was on her knees, pulling weeds from between stalks of corn. "There's a sign in the post office that says 'Food will win the war.'"

"We are doing our part." Ruth hoed around black-eyed pea plants. "We will have to carry water from the well to keep the ground moist. If only this drought would end."

The morning wore away as the sun climbed higher in the sky. The three women finished their weeding, gathered their bounty, put it in a wheel barrow, and moved to the shade of the back porch. They were gathering loads to carry inside when Ruth heard someone moving about inside the house. She signaled the other two women to silence by placing her forefinger over her lips.

A deep voice boomed from inside. "Come outta your hiding place, Faith. We know you are here."

Faith's eyes widened in terror. "Smokey Joe and his cronies have come for me. I knew sooner or later, they would." She turned to make her get away.

Mrs. Murphy grabbed her arm. "Now is not the time to run. How many cronies does he have?"

"Two, and they are both big bruisers."

Panic caught in Ruth's throat. "The two of you, go to the kitchen. Hide in the pantry. I'll go up the back stairs and get my gun." She followed the other women inside, veered left, and sped up the back stairs to her old bedroom. She no longer slept there. Now her nights were spent snuggled safely in her husband's arms.

Her pulse raced and her body was bathed in cold perspiration as she unlocked the drawer of the nightstand, and picked up the gun.

Blood-curdling screams and menacing shouts from below sent terror shivering through her. She said a silent prayer, hid the gun beneath her apron in the folds of her full skirt, and raced toward the front stairs.

Midway down, a helix of panic twisted down her spine. A massive man dragged Faith toward the front hallway. Two equally muscled men preceded him. Mrs. Murphy was nowhere in sight.

Ruth was operating on daring, adrenalin, and belief that God would protect her. She pointed her gun toward the intruder who pulled a kicking, screaming Faith along with him. "Let her go or I'll shoot you."

His grip on Faith tightened as he pulled her in front of him. "Shoot me and you hit Faith. Lay the gun down, now."

Mrs. Murphy tiptoed from the kitchen cupboard, armed with a massive iron skillet.

Ruth threatened Smokey Joe with dire consequences if he harmed Faith. They were empty threats, and she knew it. Her aim was to keep the three men occupied until Mrs. Murphy could reach Smokey Joe with her skillet.

Smokey Joe gave forth with a viciously boisterous laugh. "You don't scare me none, woman. Put the gun down."

Mrs. Murphy crept from behind, closer and closer to Smoky Joe. If any one of the three men saw her, they were all doomed. *Dear God, please let her make it.*

Ruth stooped down and very slowly laid the gun on the stair step above where she stood.

As she straightened to a standing position, Mrs. Murphy lifted the skillet high and struck Faith's captor a resounding blow to the back of his head. The crash echoed across the room like a gunshot.

Smoky Joe loosened his hold on Faith, and fell, lifeless, to the floor. Blood oozed from the wound on the back of his head.

The two men accompanying him raced for the front door and safety.

Ruth's legs refused to support her. She collapsed onto a stair step.

Mrs. Murphy sat on a kitchen chair and put the bloody skillet on the table. "Someone should call the police."

It came to Ruth, like a bolt from the blue, she didn't know Mrs. Murphy's given name. "What is your name, your given name? I can't call someone who saved my life Mrs. Murphy."

Mrs. Murphy scowled. "My name is Bessie Beulah. Don't dare address me by either of them. Bessie and Beulah are suitable labels for cows, but not for human beings."

Despite the fact that she was shaking and scared out of wits, Ruth smiled. "Mrs. Murphy it is."

Mrs. Murphy turned her attention to Faith. "Are you hurt?"

Faith sat on the floor, rubbing her arms. "No, not physically. I was scared within an inch of my life."

Ruth grabbed the stair bannister, and pulled herself to her feet. "I'll call the police."

Ruth talked personally to Police Chief Norman. She told him what happened, and urged him to get there as soon as possible.

"I will send someone over immediately."

Ruth didn't want "someone". She wanted the chief himself, and she said so, most emphatically, before adding, "I will expect you in fifteen minutes."

Chief Norman made it in twenty. He was a tall, heavy-set man with red hair and a ruddy face. He viewed the unconscious man on the floor. "So Smoky Joe finally met his match. Which one of you ladies did him in?"

Mrs. Murphy shifted in her chair. "I did. Is he dead?"

Chief Norman stooped and felt Smoky Joe's pulse. "Only the good die young. Old Smoky is still very much with us." He stood and ran his fingers through his hair. "Tell me what happened here." He sat beside Mrs. Murphy, took a pad from his shirt pocket, and retrieved a pencil from behind his ear.

Faith sat across from Mrs. Murphy. "Smoky Joe and his two buddies tried to kidnap me."

Chief Norman narrowed his eyes and stared at the young woman who sat across from him. "I know Smoky Joe and his thug friends. There is only one reason they would come after you. Are you one of Miss Lola's girls?"

Ruth's temper exploded into a hundred fiery fragments. She shooed Faith from her chair. "Sit over by Mrs. Murphy."

Chief Norman objected. "I still have a few things to say to that young lady."

Ruth's gaze locked into the chief's surprised stare. "Not before I say some things to you."

Chief Norman barked, "Just a minute--"

Ruth grasped the sides of the table and leaned forward. "Shut up!"

Much to her surprise, the chief obeyed. His face was as red as a turkey gobbler's snout.

Ruth lowered her voice to a threatening growl. "What kind of police officer are you? I called you because three men broke into my home and tried to kidnap my employee." She took a deep breath.

Chief Norman opened his mouth to speak.

Ruth raised one hand. "I'm not finished yet. Instead of offering some assurance you will catch and punish these men, you have the unmitigated gall to interrogate my employee as if she were a criminal. If you know so much about Miss Lola and her so called fun house, why haven't you done something about that den of iniquity long before now?"

Chief Norman lowered his head. "Until now, we haven't had enough evidence to arrest Smoky Joe. Miss Lola's place is out of the city limits. I have no jurisdiction there. Right now it's under quarantine. Over half of the people there have the flu."

Ruth shook her head. "Excuses, excuses. How much does Miss Lola pay you to leave her alone?"

The red on Chief Norman's face spread to his ears and blotched his neck. "You should be careful how you throw accusations around."

Henry came down the hall and stood in the doorway. "Mrs. Wallace next door called and said the police chief was at my house. What happened?"

Smoky Joe stirred and moaned. He lay in an ever-widening puddle of blood. Henry stared down at him. "What happened to this man?"

Ruth grinned. "He did battle with Mrs. Murphy's skillet. The skillet won."

Henry's voice was deep and authoritative. He pointed toward Smoky Joe as he spoke to Chief Norman. "If that criminal is on my kitchen floor when my children return from school, you will answer to me."

Chief Norman jumped to his feet. "If I may use your telephone, I will call for a paddy wagon, now."

Henry nodded toward the front parlor. "Do it, and don't fool around."

With Henry's arrival, Chief Norman's attitude did a complete about face. After the arrival of the paddy wagon, and the departure of a moaning, complaining Smoky Joe, he politely asked everyone to be seated around the kitchen table. "I have to file a report. It's necessary that I ask each of you a few questions."

Henry took command of the situation. "Before you begin, I have something to say. I am deeply disturbed that three criminals could break into my home and threaten my family."

"It won't happen again." Chief Norman assured him. He questioned the women, this time in a much more subdued manner. He ended by saying, "Thank you for your cooperation. I will post a patrolman in front of your house until Smokey Joe's two henchmen are apprehended."

Henry escorted him outside. The two men stood on the front porch and talked for a short time.

They were interrupted by the children coming from school, shouting their surprise at seeing Henry at home so early in the afternoon and asking why a policeman was on their front porch.

"He's a friend," Henry said. "Get inside and say hello to your mama."

It took a while, but things finally settled down. Mrs. Murphy made dinner. Ruth and Faith brought their garden vegetables into the house, and began the long procedure of storing them in proper places.

Henry returned to the kitchen and helped the children with their homework.

Despite the hectic happenings of the day, Ruth felt more at peace than she had in a long time. She had so much to tell Henry, but not in the presence of the children. She smiled at him from across the room. He winked one eye and smiled back at her.

Chapter Twenty-Five

Cedar Gap, Texas
Sunday Morning
July 28th, 1918

A hot, humid summer limped by, slowly, but surely. The flu epidemic lessened, but refused to go away. Churches in the town stopped services until further notice. Stores were open only a few hours a day, three days a week. City parks, usually filled with summer picnickers, were closed. Many people wore masks when they went out in public.

After their brush with Smoky Joe and his cohorts, Ruth set aside a time each morning for a family devotional period. "We have so much to be thankful for."

Faith and Mrs. Murphy agreed. After a while their time together each morning fell into a pattern. In turn each woman read a chapter from the Bible after which they discussed the scripture read. Ruth was more and more amazed at Mrs. Murphy's knowledge of the Bible and its teachings. By the time the middle of July rolled around, Mrs. Murphy became the teacher, with Ruth and Faith her willing pupils.

Early one Sunday morning, as the trio sat around the kitchen table with open Bibles before them, Henry came into the room. "I have accepted Mrs. Murphy's invitation to join your Bible study, if no one objects."

Ruth wanted to shout for joy. She patted the seat of the chair next to her. "We are delighted. Sit here, by me."

Faith echoed Ruth's welcome before saying, "Today Mrs. Murphy is reading from the Psalms. Do you know what a Psalm is?"

"I think I know the connotation the word carries." Faith's puzzled look made Henry explain. "I know the meaning of the word."

Mrs. Murphy looked at him over the top of her glasses. "It's about time you showed up. Let's get on with our reading from the One Hundredth Psalm. Will you read the Psalm, Mr. Jarrett?"

Ruth looked away to hide a fugitive smile. What a difference time made in her relationship with this woman. *Thank you, God.*

Ruth scooted her chair closer to Henry, and pushed her Bible nearer to him. "You can read from my Bible."

If Henry was surprised, he didn't show it. He cleared his throat and began:

Make a joyful noise unto the Lord, all ye lands. Serve the Lord with gladness: come before his presence with singing. Know ye that the Lord he is God: It is he that hath made us, and not we ourselves: we are his people and the sheep of his pasture. (Psalms 100; verses1-3 KJV)

Mrs. Murphy interrupted to say, "Despite the war and the sickness around us, we can rest in the knowledge that we belong to God, and that He cares for us. We can find comfort in those words."

Faith said, "For a long time I was a lost sheep. I found my way to safety and I thank Him every day."

Ruth spoke. "God leads His children where He wants them to be. He led me to Henry and the children. I thank Him for guiding me here."

Mrs. Murphy smiled. "There is an old hymn that says, '*God leads His dear children along -- Some through the water, some through the flood. Some through great sorrow, but all through the blood.*'" She nodded her head toward Henry. "Go on."

Henry returned her nod, and continued:

Enter into his gates with thanksgiving, and into his courts with praise: be thankful unto him, and bless his name. For the Lord is good; his mercy is everlasting; and his truth endureth to all generations. (Psalms 100; verses 5 and 6, KJV)

Mrs. Murphy reached across the table and motioned for Henry to hold her hand. Ruth took his other hand, then offered her remaining hand to Faith. Mrs. Murphy took Faith's other hand, and bowed her head. "Let's go to the Lord in prayer. Mrs. Jarrett, will you lead us?"

Ruth closed her eyes and poured her heart out to her Heavenly Father. Her prayer was short, but heartfelt. She said "Amen," and lifted her head.

Henry squeezed her hand before he let go.

Ruth's heart overflowed with gratitude. "Will you worship with us again?"

Henry stood. "I will, and that's a promise."

*****

Cedar Gap, Texas
Friday Morning
September 27th, 1918

The weather was warm and balmy, but a hint of autumn hung in the air.

Ruth watched the postman walk away before retrieving her mail.

She had a letter from Flossie. She sat at the kitchen table, tore it open and read:

Dear Friend,

Mr. Johnson died two weeks ago. His bad leg, on top of catching the flu, was more than he could take. Little Ruby will never know her papa. That makes me sad.

My sister, the one that had a baby and ain't married, and me, run the farm now. Papa has lost his mind. He sleeps most of the time. Mama is sick. I hope it ain't the flu.

I am glad you and your husband got together.
Write to me soon and God bless you.

Your friend,
Flossie

Ruth slipped the letter back into the envelope. She would write Flossie later today, and express her sympathy. She felt guilty about her own happiness when there was so much sorrow in the world.

A knock sounded at the front door.

Mrs. Murphy hurried to open it.

An out-of-breath young man gasped, as he followed Mrs. Murphy into the kitchen. "I have a message from Dr. Mullins for Mrs. Ruth Jarrett."

Ruth laid Flossie's letter aside, and came to stand beside Mrs. Murphy. "I'm Mrs. Jarrett."

"Dr. Mullins says you should come, quick. He says it's an emergency."

Ruth reached for her hat. "Where is Dr. Mullins?"

"He's at his clinic." The young man raced toward the street. "I'll tell his nurse you are on your way."

Ruth raced after him as she called over her shoulder to Mrs. Murphy, "Take care of things here. I should return soon." Something was terribly amiss. Dr. Mullins would not send for her if there wasn't. A dozen diverse and frightening thoughts ran through her mind.

Chapter Twenty-Six

Cedar Gap, Texas
Friday Noon
September 27th, 1918

Ruth turned the corner onto Main Street. Dr. Mullins's clinic came into view, if indeed it could be called a clinic. It was once the only school in Cedar Gap. It was abandoned in 1910. Dr. Mullins bought it in 1912. Its location was in the center of town. Its structure and floor plan, an assembly room that opened into a wide hall with two class rooms on either side, made converting it to a clinic as well as his residence, a simple procedure. Ruth doubted the two rooms reserved for patients had ever both been occupied at the same time. Most women gave birth at home. Older citizens of Cedar Gap and the surrounding area used their own remedies for minor illnesses. Severe cases demanding surgery were referred to the hospital in Waco. Only cuts needing stitches, broken limbs, minor burns, and other trivial emergencies made it to *Dr. Mullins's Medical Clinic.*

She pulled the front door open and hurried to the receptionist's desk. After she caught her breath, she told Betty Welch, who was behind the desk, "Dr. Mullins sent for me. He says it's an emergency."

Betty came from behind the desk and hurried down the hall. "This way. I am so glad you are here. We are doing the best we can, but we are not trained nurses. We mostly follow Dr. Mullins's directions." Before Ruth could ask questions, she opened the door to one of the patient rooms, and stepped back.

Ruth entered to see Dr. Mullins lying in one of the two beds in the room. A second look told her that he was a sick man. He tried to raise his head, and failed. "At last, you are here."

Ruth opened drawers in the chest between the beds, found a face mask, and put it on. "You have the three-day fever. Now you also have a nurse. I will take care of you until you recover." She turned to give directions to Betty. The woman was nowhere in sight.

Dr. Mullins moaned, "Ruth, please."

Ruth turned back toward Dr. Mullins's bed.

He motioned with one finger. "Come nearer, but not too near."

Ruth disregarded his statement, came to stand beside his bed, and laid her cool hand on his feverish brow. His skin was blue. He gasped as he spoke. "Listen to me. I don't have much time. I am dying."

"No," Ruth cried. Even as she objected, she suspected his diagnosis was correct.

"*Please, Ruth,* listen to me. I have the flu." He was seized by a wrenching fit of coughing.

Ruth covered his shivering body with the blanket folded and lying on the foot of the bed. She tucked it under his neck. "Don't try to talk."

"I must," Dr. Mullins said. "I am an old man with a bad heart, kidney problems, and a severe case of the flu. I don't have much time left."

This can't be happening. Ruth swallowed her fear and asked, "What do you want me to do?" If he hadn't called her here to nurse him, what did he want?

With great effort, as chills shivered through his body, Dr. Mullins whispered, "When I go, there will be no available doctor in a fifty mile radius of this little town." Another fit of coughing seized the old man. His chest heaved and his body twisted. When he could get his breath again, he croaked, "You must keep my office open, and care for emergencies that arise."

Ruth was no doctor. She wasn't even an experienced nurse. She panicked. "I will find a doctor to take your place." *No one could take Dr. Mullins's place.*

Dr. Mullins voice rattled in his throat. "That's impossible. Many of the doctors in this area have succumbed to the flu." Froth bubbled from the doctor's mouth. He wiped it away with his hand. "The ones left have more cases than they can handle." Blood trickled from one side of his mouth. "Promise me, girl, that you will take care of emergencies, and do what you can for flu patients." His breath came in heaving gasps. "This epidemic will get worse before it gets better. When I am out of this room scrub it down with disinfectant. *Promise me!*"

Ruth had once prayed to God to send her to a place she was needed. An old adage ran through her mind. *Be careful what you pray for, you just might get it.* "I promise I will do my best." *Dear God, I am going to need your guiding hand.* She rang the call bell and waited for Betty to appear.

Blood flowed from both sides of Dr. Mullins's mouth, and out his ears. It ran in streams onto his pillow and flowed onto his sheet. She felt for a pulse. There was none. She laid her fingers alongside his neck. Nothing, the old man was dead.

Not Betty, but a middle-aged woman dressed in a nurse's uniform stuck her head through the door. "Yes, Ma'am?"

Ruth snapped, "Call the undertaker to pick up Dr. Mullins's body, and come back here with lots of disinfectant. We must scrub down this room."

The woman stood staring at her. "Is Dr. Mullins dead?"

"Yes." Ruth laid Dr. Mullins's arm across his chest and with her other hand closed his eyes. He was with his Letty now, and in the presence of his Savior.

The woman stood like a stone statue. "Dr. Mullins can't be dead."

Ruth shook her head. "Dr. Mullins is very dead. *Move.*"

The woman ran like a scared rabbit, chanting, "Yes, Ma'am," over and over as she sped away.

Ruth pulled a sheet over Dr. Mullins's face, and left the room, closing the door behind her.

Half-way down the hall, she met the woman she sent for disinfectant. "Did you call the undertaker?" As an afterthought, she asked, "What is your name?"

"I'm Zeta Durham. Call me Zeta. The undertaker will be here, but it will be a while. He has two calls ahead of us."

A sense of foreboding lodged in Ruth's stomach. *Please, dear Jesus, help me.* The first thing she must do was take charge of the clinic, which meant she must find the key to the front door.

She found a large ring of keys in the top drawer of Dr. Mullins's desk. Ruth secured the front door after hanging a sign on it that read *New hours 10:00 A. M. to 4:00 P. M. Monday-Friday*

She waited until the undertaker came for Dr. Mullins's body before she told Zeta to bring the clinic staff to the waiting room. "Tell them it's important."

"We don't have much of a staff," Zeta told her. "Just me and Betty, and Leland Young. Enos Newby is our handyman and general flunky."

Zeta quickly assembled them. They sat in a semicircle in ancient chairs that had to be relics from the old school. Each one looked with anxious expressions toward the tall woman who stood before them.

Ruth assessed each person. Leland Young was that, young. She guessed his age to be no more than nineteen or twenty. He wore white pants and an over blouse with short sleeves and a round neckline. She riveted her glance into his dark eyes. "What is your position here, Mr. Young?"

Leland didn't flinch. His gaze locked into hers. "I am -- I was -- Dr. Mullins's assistant. I am -- I was, studying medicine under him."

"You are now my assistant," Ruth informed him.

She moved next to Zeta and Betty. "What are your jobs here, ladies?" She stood waiting for one of them to speak.

After a spate of silence, Zeta drew a deep breath. "I suppose you could say I am Leland's assistant."

Betty lifted her hand as if she was in grammar school. "I'm Zeta's assistant, sometimes. Sometimes I'm the receptionist."

Enos chuckled. "You don't need to ask. I'm assistant to the assistant's assistant. I do might near everything around here that nobody else will do."

Ruth smiled. The old man had a sense of humor. He would need it before this was over. She pulled a chair to the center of the semicircle, and sat down. "Dr. Mullins is gone, but you all know that. We are faced with an epidemic of a deadly strain of flu. There is no doctor we can call to help us. The siege ahead of us is dangerous, maybe deadly. Dr. Mullins asked me to take over his offices and practice. I promised him I would. I am not a doctor. I am a registered nurse. I will do the best I can. If you elect to stay with me, I will be grateful. If you don't, you are free to leave and no one will think the worse of you for going."

Enos scratched the side of his balding head. "I reckon I'll stay."

Leland nodded his head. "I'll stay."

Ruth relaxed, a little. "Thank you."

Zeta stared at her hands that lay clasped in her lap. "I'm with you, Mrs. Jarrett."

"Thank you, Zeta, and my name is Ruth."

Betty grinned. "My old man will probably pitch a hissy-fit, but I'll stay, Miss Ruth."

Not once had Ruth thought of how Henry would react to her committing to running Dr. Mullins's clinic. *Lord, please make him understand.*

"Where do we go from here," Leland asked as he stood and pushed his chair against the wall.

That was a good question. Ruth wished she knew the answer. "We can start by washing down the room Dr. Mullins was in with disinfectant. From this day forward, we should all wear face masks."

As she walked home, Ruth rehearsed in her mind what she would tell Henry about her newly-acquired position as head nurse of *Dr. Mullins's Medical Clinic.* Time would tell what lay ahead. Meanwhile she would take one day at a time and rely on her Heavenly Father to guide her.

Chapter Twenty-Seven

Cedar Gap, Texas
Friday Night
September 27th, 1918

Through dinner Ruth was preoccupied.

Henry noticed her inattentive state. "Is something troubling you, my dear?"

Ruth studied her full plate of food. "We will talk about it later."

Mrs. Murphy leaned across the table and pointed her fork in Ruth's direction. "Eat your dinner. I don't know what happened when you visited Dr. Mullins, but you have been upset since you returned."

Henry laid his knife across his plate. "What happened?"

Ruth pushed her fork through her mashed potatoes. "I'll tell you later."

Jake, perceptive as always, said, "Aunt Mama doesn't want us to hear."

Joe and Rosie asked in unison, "Why not?"

"'Cause, dummies, it's about grown-up stuff."

All three children began talking at once.

Henry stood. His commanding presence was enough to silence the three. He addressed Faith. "Miss Faith, will you put the children to bed tonight?"

"I'll be glad to, sir."

Henry extended his hand in Ruth's direction. "Come along, my dear. It's time we had a talk."

Once inside their bedroom, Henry led Ruth to the love seat in the corner then pulled her down beside him. He took both her hands in his.

Before he had time to ask questions, Ruth uttered in a flat monotone, "Dr. Mullins died this afternoon."

Henry wrapped his arms around her. "The flu?"

Ruth nodded before burying her head in his shoulder. "Why would God take him when this community needs him so badly?"

Henry offered her his handkerchief. "Are you questioning God?"

Ruth straightened and wiped tears from her eyes. "I was, but I shouldn't. With His help, I won't again. God doesn't make mistakes." Through her repenting grief, one fact stood clear. Henry spoke as if he believed there was a God. "Do you believe there is a God?"

Henry stood and walked across the floor before turning to face her. "I do. My belief came gradually. It began when I attended your Bible studies. I started to read and study more. Progressively, it was revealed to me that Jesus was either the biggest liar who ever walked the face of this earth or the true son of God. I looked around me and saw not only the beauty and vastness of the world, but the change He makes in individual lives. The only logical conclusion is He is God's son and as such both God and man."

Ruth's heart overflowed with joy. "Have you confessed your belief in Him and asked Him to forgive you of your sins?"

"I would like to do that with you at my side."

Ruth slipped off the love seat and fell to her knees. "Come and kneel beside me."

Henry obeyed. "This is our first prayer together. I will remember it always." He held her hand and bowed his head. "Dear Jesus, I know I am a sinner. I ask you to forgive me of those many sins and welcome me into your kingdom as one of your redeemed children. Amen."

Ruth prayed a prayer of joy and thanksgiving. "Praise you, Jesus, for pouring out your blessings on me and my family." Tears choked in her throat. She could say no more. "Amen."

She scrambled onto the loveseat and patted the space beside her. "The church is closed because of the flu epidemic. It may be sometime before we can attend as a family, but we can have our own worship service, here at home."

Henry sat beside her. "As of next Monday the schools in this district will be closed. Before they are, you should speak to the children's teachers. Get copies of their curricula. We will teach them at home."

Ruth moved to her corner of the loveseat. "Dr. Mullins called me to the clinic today because he knew he was dying. I watched him go and it was horrible." She folded her arms across her breast and shuddered. "This flu is a vicious killer."

Henry's eyes filled with compassion. "It's taking its toll all over the world. Why did Dr. Mullins send for you if he knew he was dying?"

Ruth took a deep breath and expelled it slowly. "He wants me to run his clinic."

Henry's eyes widened in surprise. "You are not a doctor."

Ruth knew that, all too well. "I am the nearest person in Cedar Gap to a doctor. The flu has taken many of the doctors in this area. The others are overloaded with patients."

Henry moved nearer. "I have no doubt what your answer was."

"How could I refuse?" Ruth breathed a sigh of relief. He did understand.

Henry gathered her in a close embrace. "You couldn't, no more than I can forbid you to take on such a danger-filled task."

Until this moment, Ruth had not realized how afraid she was of what his answer might be. "What about the children? Who will teach them?"

Henry kissed her cheek. "I will. Starting next week I will close the bank three days a week. We don't have many people coming in now." He moved his lips to cover hers.

How much she loved this man. How proud she was of him for humbling himself to ask Jesus for forgiveness. How dark and foreboding the future loomed ahead of them. She closed her mind to all tomorrows. This now she would enjoy the comfort of her husband's close embrace.

*****

The next morning over breakfast Ruth explained that she would be running D. Mullins's clinic until further notice.

Mrs. Murphy was not fooled. "Dr. Mullins passed away in your presence yesterday, didn't he?"

Ruth nodded. "Yes. With his dying breath, he asked me to carry on for him."

Faith reached across the table and caught Ruth's hand in hers. "What do you want us to do to help?"

Ruth knew one thing for sure. "You must isolate yourselves as much as possible. Don't let anyone into the house. No one knows what causes this flu, therefore no one knows how to cure it. If any of you comes down with a fever, call me at the clinic immediately."

Mrs. Murphy shook her head. "The folks in this part of the world don't go to doctors. I doubt they would consider a nurse any better. They go to druggists, folk healers, or faith healers, or rely on their own remedies."

What an opportunity for those who made and sold quack remedies. Ruth pressed her fingertips to her temples, and rubbed gently. "I will treat those who do come to me. Some will need my help with minor accidents or illnesses."

Henry shoved his coffee cup from him. "You have just acquired a new assistant -- me."

Surprise silenced Ruth long enough for Mrs. Murphy to say. "Mr. Jarrett, you are a prince of a man."

Ruth agreed. That was reason enough not to want him exposed to the flu every day for she didn't know how long. "That's kind of you, Mr. Jarrett, but as I recall, you have a job, teaching the children."

Faith stood and stacked dishes. "I can teach the children. I wanted to be a teacher before -- once. I graduated at the top of my high school senior class."

"It's settled then," Henry said.

She had been out maneuvered. Ruth acquiesced gracefully. "Thank you, Faith. That is most gracious of you." The young woman's reference to her education came as a surprise. Faith seldom spoke of her past.

"Thank *you,*" Faith answered, as she put her dishes in the sink, and turned to go. "Excuse me. I must get the children up and see to their breakfast."

"I'll make their breakfast," Mrs. Murphy called after Faith as she exited the room.

Henry stood and offered Ruth his hand. "Come along, my dear. It is time we began our day."

Ruth stood, and put her hand in his. She was not happy about the events of the morning. So many thoughts ran through her mind. How would Henry fare in the stark, labor intensive atmosphere of a medical clinic? "The clinic isn't open on Saturday."

"All the better," Henry replied. "You can acquaint me with my duties so I will be prepared for Monday."

Ruth had no idea what his duties would be. She wasn't even sure of what she would be required to do. "Do you think Faith can handle tutoring the children?"

"She will manage."

Ruth was not so sure. Faith's past was shrouded in mystery. Ruth made a silent vow as she followed Henry down the hall. *I will solve that mystery, sooner or later.*

Chapter Twenty-Eight

Cedar Gap, Texas
Monday Morning
October 7th, 1918

Ruth unlocked the front door of the clinic and stepped inside. Henry followed her. She asked him, "How are you managing?"

Henry smiled. "I can cope. Stop worrying about me. You already have more than enough on your mind."

That was an understatement. The last nine days had been hectic. Ruth spent much of that time drilling into Betty, Zeta, and even Leland, the importance of isolating flu patients, disinfecting rooms, surfaces, and eating utensils, washing their hands often and thoroughly, and wearing a face mask at all times.

Flu cases multiplied in geometric proportion. It soon became apparent they could not begin to treat all those asking for help. Ruth broke the staff into two teams. Leland and Zeta made one team. They drove Dr. Mullins's buggy to make their rounds. She and Henry were the other team. They traveled in Henry's Model T. Betty was assigned to stay at the clinic to take care of minor emergencies and keep a list of people coming into the clinic reporting friends or relatives with the flu.

Ruth was holding their regular morning staff meeting, discussing procedures and answering questions when ten-year-old Aaron Crawford came tearing into the room. "Come quick, Miz. Jarrett. It's Mama's time. She's trying to have her baby, and she can't."

Ruth grabbed Dr. Mullins's little black bag, which she now claimed as her own, took Aaron's hand, and nodded to Henry. "Let's go. Leland, carry on."

In less than ten minutes they were across town and pulling into the drive of a run-down three-room house. Blood-curdling screams, painful to hear, sounded from inside and echoed across the neighborhood.

"That's Mama." Aaron put his hands over his ears and begged, "Please help her, Miz. Jarrett."

Ruth was out of the car and following Henry up the walk. "Find your papa and bring him home."

They entered the front room to find a woman lying on the bed in a pool of blood. Her screams told of her excruciating pain. Ruth dropped her bag and sterilized her hands before beginning her examination. *Dear God, help me.* The baby was breech. Its tiny behind protruded from its mama. The look on Henry's face was one of stark terror. "What do you want me to do?"

"Boil some water, find some clean towels, rags, or whatever, and bring them to me. Bring a paper bag if you can find one."

The screaming ceased momentarily. Ruth sat at the foot of the bed and kneaded Mrs. Crawford's stomach. "Hang on, I'm here to help you."

Three children came from the other room. The tallest one, and the only girl asked, "Is Mama going to die?"

I pray not. "Be a good girl. Go back into your room, close the door, and take care of your brothers."

The three disappeared as Mrs. Crawford let out another ear-splitting scream.

"Push." Ruth said.

The pain pushed the baby far enough out for Ruth to use her fingers to reach inside through the slime and blood and slip one of the baby's legs outside the mama's body. She was sweating profusely and her heart beat double time. She moved her hand to the other side of the baby and very carefully pulled the other leg outside the mother's body. She closed her ears to the mama's pitiful screams. Blood flowed freely. This delivery must be accomplished swiftly and carefully if she hoped to save both mother and baby.

Henry reappeared, gave Ruth two large towels, and sat a large paper bag on the floor beside the bed.

Ruth wrapped one of the towels around the baby's exposed buttocks.

Another pain and another heart rending scream pushed the baby out far enough for Ruth to see its back. Oh, so carefully, she wrapped another towel around its slick, bloody body. She grasped the baby with both hands and carefully rotated its little body until she could feel the elbow of one of its tiny arms. She reached inside and gently pulled the right arm free before once more rotating the baby, and freeing the left arm.

Two more screams and two more pushes brought the baby's shoulders into view. Ruth placed her right hand on its upper back. With her left hand, she elevated the baby, oh so slightly before she moved her fingers to touch its chin. With one last excursing pain and another blood-curdling scream, he slid free. She cut and tied the navel cord and wrapped the baby in another towel. "Mrs. Crawford, you have a fine boy."

The exhausted woman rested her head on her pillow and smiled. "Another boy, that's just what I needed." Ruth gave the baby to Henry. "Use some of the water you heated to clean him up, bring him back to his mother, and then fetch a basin of warm water in here. I need to attend to Mrs. Crawford."

Henry disappeared into the kitchen.

Ruth delivered the afterbirth, and put it in to the paper bag before examining Mrs. Crawford. Except for some tears, she had fared well. "I'm going to make a few stitches. It will hurt, but it must be done."

Mrs. Crawford smiled. "After what I've been through, what are a few stitches?"

Ruth wiped away blood and did an extensive repair job on Mrs. Crawford. "You have lost a tremendous amount of blood. You should stay in bed for a while. Is there someone who can come and stay with you for a week or so?"

Henry reappeared with the clean baby wrapped in a clean towel. "Your water will be here shortly." He laid the baby in Mrs. Crawford's arms.

Ruth put disinfectant into the basin and poured it over Mrs. Crawford's stitches. "Feed him, he's hungry."

Aaron came through the door followed by two women, one elderly, the other near the age of Mrs. Crawford. "Papa's boss wouldn't let him leave. I fetched Aunt Lizzie and Grandma."

Ruth covered Mrs. Crawford with her bloody sheet. "You did a good job. Go now and stay with your brothers and your sister."

Aaron asked, as he made a reluctant retreat, "Is Mama okay?"

"Your mama is going to be fine and you have a new brother."

Aaron let out a loud whoop. "Another boy? Goodie."

Aunt Lizzie kissed her sister and inspected the baby. "He is a big one."

Grandma hovered over Mrs. Crawford. "Aaron might near scared us to death saying you couldn't have the baby. Are you going to be all right?"

"I'm going to be fine, thanks to Nurse Jarrett and her husband. They got here in time to save us both."

Ruth sat in a chair. Inside she was shaking like a leaf in a windstorm. "Mrs. Crawford's bed should be changed and she could use some food. She lost a lot of blood. Thank God the bleeding has stopped. She should stay in bed for at least a week, maybe two."

Grandma held the baby in her arms. "Don't you worry none, Nurse Jarrett, me and Lizzie will take care of both baby and mama."

Aunt Lizzie took the baby from his grandmother's arms. "What are you going to name him"?

Mrs. Crawford smiled. "His name is Henry Jarrett Crawford."

Henry gulped and dropped into a chair in the far corner of the room. "Mrs. Crawford, I am honored that you would name your son after me."

"If you hadn't been here I might not have a son to name. I might not be here myself."

Ruth picked up her bag. "We must go. Send Aaron if you need us. Who is your husband's employee?"

"He works at the lumber yard," Mrs. Crawford replied before

saying. "If this is about the money we owe you--"

Ruth interrupted, "You don't owe us a dime."

Grandma raised her bushy gray eyebrows. "Why not?"

Ruth moved toward the door. "Henry Jarrett Crawford is the first baby I ever delivered. I don't charge for first babies."

Amid thanks and bless you from the three women, Ruth and Henry shut the door and walked toward the car. They were far down the road when Ruth said, "Stop by the lumber yard."

Henry began, "Ruth--"

"I want to tell Mr. Crawford his wife is all right."

Henry cast a quick glance in her direction. "Your uniform is splattered with blood. You look like you were in a fist fight."

Ruth slowly and distinctly pronounced each word. "Stop at the lumber yard."

Henry shrugged. "If you say so, but I think--"

Ruth changed the subject. "I never delivered a baby before. When I saw he was breech, I almost panicked. The lives of two human beings were in my hands. I asked God for help, and a sudden calm settled over me. I forgot everything except the astounding thought that I had been trusted with the wondrous privilege of bringing a new life into the world. God helped me make a safe delivery and I praise Him for it."

Henry slowed to make a turn toward the lumber yard. "I was praying too."

Ruth turned to stare at him. "You were?"

"Indeed I was. Ruth, you never cease to amaze me. Most women I know would have run at the sight of that baby stuck inside his mother."

Ruth's heart lifted with his praise. "That thought never entered my mind. My calling is to heal the sick. Don't forget to stop at the lumber yard."

Henry stopped before the lumber yard office and opened his car door.

Ruth put her hand on his arm. "You don't have to come with me." She noticed, for the first time, how disheveled he was. "You look more like a bum than a banker." She repeated words she had heard him say so many times before. "You do have an image to maintain."

Henry chuckled. "I will sacrifice my image to watch what happens when you tear into Mr. Crawford's boss."

"I never said--" Ruth opened her car door and stepped to the ground.

Henry took her arm. He was still smiling when he opened the lumber yard door for his wife. "Let's go."

In short order, Ruth asked to see Mr. Crawford. When he appeared, she assured him his wife was doing well, and that he had another healthy son.

He thanked her, and with an unsure look at the man who called him, turned and left.

Ruth then demanded to see the lumber yard's owner.

"I am the manager," the man behind the counter said. "You can talk to me."

Ruth banged on the counter. "You, sir, are not worthy of my attention. Fetch the owner!" Her shout echoed through the room.

The man scooted to do her bidding.

Henry sat on a pile of lumber, smiled, and waited.

Chapter Twenty-Nine

Cedar Gap, Texas
Monday
November 18th, 1918

The last month had been hectic. The news of Ruth's safe delivery of the Crawford baby spread like wild fire. Many people in the community, who were previously reluctant to acknowledge her medical help and advice, accepted it now with gratitude. That was both a blessing and a challenge. The clinic's case load doubled.

November the eleventh the war ended. The staff rejoiced in that news then went on with their battle against an unseen, unrelenting enemy. Ruth wondered if the siege would ever end. She clung to the promise that God would not make her burden too heavy to bear.

Each morning the staff gathered in Dr. Mullins's office and prayed for strength for that day. "Today is all we can expect," Ruth told her co-workers. "Our chances of contacting the flu are far above average, but with God's help, we will persist." In the beginning she lived with the fear that one, or all of her helpers, would desert her. After a while she came to know that they were as dedicated to their duty as she was to hers. *Thank you, God, for sending me such a devoted team.*

Henry remained her faithful and staunch ally. He was also wise in ways she would never have thought to be. In mid-October he suggested the entire staff move into Dr. Mullins's living quarters. "We shouldn't continue to expose our families to the flu."

The quarters were cramped. Ruth and Henry slept in Dr. Mullins's bedroom. Leland and Henry put up two hospital beds in his living room, Zeta and Betty slept there. Leland and Enos shared one of the patient rooms. Betty took over the task of cooking meals. "I have the easy job around here," she said. "Another chore won't be too much."

Ruth missed her family, even Mrs. Murphy. She had grown quite fond of the woman she once considered her enemy. Faith reported by telephone that the children were doing well with their lessons. The children promised they would continue to study and be good students.

Once again, life settled into a routine. This time it was a grueling one. Each morning Ruth and Henry called on the sickest patients. Some recovered, some didn't. Some who did recover from the flu, had relapses or fell victim to pneumonia, and died. Ruth had never felt so inadequate. There was no cure for the flu. All she could do was see those who were sickest on a regular basis and offer advice. Flu patients needed a good diet, rest, and proper care. Often entire families fell ill at the same time. Shortage of nurses and doctors made it impossible to call in help to care for them. Many of her patients died from dehydration, starvation, and poor care.

Unlike many of the larger cities who refused to shut down war rallies and public transportation systems until they were forced to do so, Cedar Gap closed schools and businesses in early October. Essentials such as groceries and feed for livestock were ordered by telephone and set outside the stores for customers to pick up.

Rawlins' Funeral Parlor was overwhelmed with dead bodies. At Ruth's insistence they buried many of them in common graves. This was only after Ruth explained that accumulation of corpses of flu victims could start a secondary epidemic caused by organisms that lived in dead flesh.

The most heartbreaking thing Ruth dealt with was that a majority of her flu victims were so young. Most of them were in their twenties to early thirties. She knew she shouldn't, but she often asked God why He permitted such tragedies. She could see no reason for such waste of human potential.

The morning of November eighteenth Ruth received a frantic call from Jason. "Can you come, please? Clara and Jasper have both come down with the flu. I think Clara is dying."

Ruth's calm voice belied the fear that kicked in her stomach. "Hold on, Jason. We will be there soon. Take Leon to another part of the house. Isolate him from Clara and Jasper. Raise the windows and let plenty of fresh air into the room where he is."

"What about Clara and Jasper? What can I do for them?" Fear underlined every word Jason spoke.

"I'll be there soon." Ruth put the telephone on its hook, grabbed her bag, and motioned to Henry. "Clara and Jasper have the flu. Let's go."

In a matter of minutes they were parking in front of Jason's house. He ran to meet them. "Come quickly. Clara is having trouble breathing."

Ruth knew the moment she saw Clara that her friend was not long for this world. She was blue. Froth gurgled from mouth. Ruth had seen these death-signs so many times before.

Henry put his arm around Jason's shoulders. "We should check on Jasper."

Jason didn't move. "Jasper doesn't need anyone. He's dead. I wrapped him in a blanket and put him in the other room. Leon is fine. He's in the kitchen with all the windows open. Clara needs me."

Ruth sent Henry a look that said, get him out of here. She didn't want Jason to see Clara die.

Henry insisted. "Perhaps we should check on Leon, just in case."

Jason refused to move. "I'm not going anywhere."

Ruth felt for Clara's pulse. There was none. She closed the dead woman's eyes, and pulled the sheet over her face. Clara would never need anyone again.

Jason burst into tears. "She's gone? She can't be. I need her. The boys need her. I love her. Bring her back!" He was hysterical with grief.

Henry bowed his head. "Pray with me, Jason. Only God can comfort you now."

Jason shook his head in negation. "I can't pray. I don't know how."

Ruth closed the gap that separated her from Jason and Henry. She completed the circle by holding the hand of each man. Bowing her head, she prayed, "Father-God. Look down on your children. Bless Jason in his time of sorrow, grief, and loss. Send him your sweet peace that passes human understanding. Keep him and Leon from harm. I pray in the blessed name of my savior, The Lord Jesus. Amen."

She lifted her head and wiped away her tears. "We have other calls to make. Can you manage?"

Jason batted tears from his eyes. "I can. I'll take Leon to Mama and Papa. They will care for him."

"Wait for a week or so," Ruth warned. "You must first be sure neither of you is coming down with the flu. Call Rawlins' Funeral Home and get Clara and Jasper's bodies out of here as soon as possible then scrub this place down with disinfectant." Her words sounded harsh in her own ears, but she needed to get her message across. She put her arms around Jason. "We must go. Can you manage alone?"

Jason nodded. "I can. Thank you for coming."

Once in Henry's car, he asked, "Where to now?"

"Jim and Ina Crocker's," Ruth answered. "He should be over his flu by now, but we haven't heard from them in some time. I want to go by their farm. Another member of the family may be ill."

Henry pulled into the street, and smiled briefly in her direction. "Go *by* the Cocker's house? Surely you jest. They live on the back side of creation."

Ruth turned to look at his strong profile. "Where else would you have a pig farm?" She shifted to stare out the car window. *I can't think about Clara now. If I do, I'll fall apart.* "We have a long day ahead of us."

The Crocker family lived in a farmhouse at the end of a deserted dirt road. Ruth knew the moment they stopped the car in the driveway that something was terribly amiss. "The house is as silent as a tomb."

Henry opened his car door. "The windows are all up and the front door is open. Stay here I will go inside and see what the problem is."

Ruth had no intention of staying here. "I'm going with you." She grabbed her black bag and got out of the car.

Henry sighed and shook his head. "Come along then." He wrinkled his nose. "This place stinks to high heaven."

Ruth clutched his arm, pulling them both to a halt. "That odor is not from the pigs."

Henry pointed to a few big flies that clung to the front screen. "Look at that, and in this weather."

Ruth heard the buzzing inside the house. "They are blow flies. The house must be full of them. They eat dead flesh." She turned and hurried toward the car. "Let's get out of here."

Henry made long strides to stay up with her. "Everyone in the house is dead. Am I right?"

Ruth nodded her head as she got into the car. "Not only dead, but contaminated." She handed Henry the car crank. "Hurry, please."

Henry wasted no time in cranking the car, and driving away.

Chill bumps covered Ruth's arms. "Drive back to Cedar Gap. The Cedar County officials must be notified immediately."

Henry pushed down on the accelerator. "How many children did they have?"

"Four." Ruth answered, "And one of them was just a baby. I should have come sooner." *Why, God? Why, why?*

Chapter Thirty

Cedar Gap, Texas
Wednesday
December 18th, 1918

With December came a lessening of flu cases. For the first time since this nightmare began, Ruth dared to hope it would soon be over. The community would be a long time recovering from the devastation it brought. Over the past two months Ruth survived by schooling herself to think only of today. She also found comfort in writing long letters to Flossie, pouring out her heart to her friend. Flossie always answered with words of comfort and hope.

Now Ruth began to contemplate the future. She thanked God daily that her family had survived.

Betty knocked on Dr. Mullins's bedroom door. "Breakfast is ready, Ruth."

"Be right there." Ruth kissed Henry on his cheek. "Time to get out of bed, sleepy head."

Henry turned and took her in his arms. "My wife is a slave driver." He kissed her long and lovingly.

How much she loved this man. As terrible as this experience had been, one good thing came from it. She and Henry were closer than they could have ever hoped to be under any ordinary circumstances. "I love you, Henry Jarrett." She slid to the side of the bed. "Breakfast is waiting."

The group ate breakfast, had their devotional, asked God to keep them this day, and prepared to begin their daily rounds. Ruth and Henry were in Henry's Model T when Betty dashed through the clinic's front door and outside. "Wait," she called as she ran to lean through the door on Ruth's side of the car. "A Mrs. Higgins called. She says her husband is bad sick and she has a fever. She wants you to come quickly. Her address is 22 Dove Street. That is way over in the fancy part of town."

As Betty ran back toward the clinic office, and Henry pulled away, Ruth said, "Arabella Higgins hates me. She must be at death's door to call on me for help."

Henry glanced briefly in her direction and smiled. "What did you do to Arabella Higgins?"

"At the first Ladies Auxiliary meeting I had at the house last February, she insulted Faith. I reacted in a most un-lady like fashion."

Henry laughed aloud. "You behaved in an un-lady like fashion? I can't believe it."

Ruth smiled and gave his arm a playful swat. "It is possible."

Henry's brows knitted together in a puzzled frown. "Arabella Higgins is acquainted with Faith? That seems strange. Did any of the other women recognize her?"

His words hit Ruth like a blow to her head. "They didn't. No one we ever came in contact with recognized Faith, except the police chief and Arabella." *There is nothing so concealed as that which lurks in plain sight.* "Why did I never think of that?" She would ponder over this later.

When they arrived at the Higgins' home, Arabella was waiting at the door. She opened it as they came onto the veranda. "Come in, and hurry."

Ruth came inside and Henry followed her. The parlor was huge, beautifully furnished, and immaculately clean.

Ruth saw no point in bandying about words. "Take us to your husband."

Arabella held onto the back of a plush sofa. "My husband died earlier this morning." She crumbled like a dried leaf and would have fallen to the floor had not Henry caught her.

Ruth opened a few downstairs doors and found a bedroom.

Henry laid Arabella atop an embroidered satin spread.

She stirred to consciousness and tried to sit.

"Lie down," Ruth told her before asking, "Why didn't you call me before your husband became so ill? I could have--"

A knock sounded on the front door.

Arabella snarled, "Shut up and answer the door."

Henry hurried to obey her command.

Same old Arabella. Ruth laid her hand on Arabella's forehead. "Try to relax. How long have you been ill?"

"Too long." Arabella's face was blue. Blood trickled from her ears. She grabbed Ruth's hand from her forehead, and held onto it. "The man at the door is my attorney. Get him in here, now."

This was no time to be concerned about legal matters. Ruth soothed the other woman as best she could. "Rest, if you can. I will stay with you." *She's dying and there is nothing I can do.*

Henry re-entered the room. He was followed by Morris Rutledge, senior partner in the town's most prestigious law firm.

Henry came to stand beside Ruth. Mr. Rutledge stopped just inside the door. He wore a surgical mask and a frightened frown.

Arabella closed her eyes. "Morris will tell you why you are here."

Ruth had one mission here, and that was to comfort a dying woman.

Mr. Rutledge's anxiety was evident. He nodded in Henry's direction. "Step outside and we can discuss the matter."

Arabella's eyes flew open. She swore before saying, "You will discuss it here." She gasped for breath, making a gurgling sound in her throat. "In my presence."

Ruth asked Henry to bring her a cool cloth to put on Arabella's forehead.

Henry turned to go.

Arabella rasped a guttural, "No."

Henry stopped as Morris Rutledge asked, "Has Mrs. Higgins survived Mr. Higgins?"

Ruth's patience was wearing thin. "Arabella says her husband is dead."

"I must ask you to check to be sure."

Arabella slipped into unconsciousness. "Check for yourself," Ruth snapped.

"I'll go." Henry volunteered.

He returned some ten minutes later carrying a basin of water and a cloth. "Mr. Higgins is in an upstairs bedroom, and I can assure you that he is very dead." He put the basin on the nightstand beside the bed.

A spasm of coughing seized Arabella. Blood spewed from her mouth before her cough altered to a rattle deep in her chest. The rattle faded to a deadly silence.

Ruth didn't bother to feel for a pulse. She had played out this scenario too many times before. Arabella Higgins was dead.

She closed the deceased woman's eyes and pulled a portion of the lovely satin spread over her.

Morris Rutledge shifted his briefcase from his right hand to his left. "Can we get out of here now? I have something important to tell you."

Ruth couldn't imagine what Mr. Rutledge had to say, but she knew she wanted to hear it. "We can sit on the veranda."

The frightened attorney scooted into the parlor ahead of Ruth and Henry. "The sooner I get there, the better I will feel."

Henry caught up to him. " "Wise choice even though it's near freezing out there."

Mr. Rutledge opened the front door. "I hope it is cold enough to freeze germs."

Ruth and Henry grabbed their coats and followed him outside.

The trio sat in three of the rocking chairs that lined the wide wrap around veranda. Ruth stuffed her hands into her coat pockets. "Say what you have to say. It's freezing out here."

Mr. Rutledge opened his brief case and extracted a long official-looking envelope from inside. "Mrs. Higgins called me to her home yesterday. She said her husband had fallen ill, and some changes must be made in her will. I was reluctant to come, what with the flu still striking so many people down. She pleaded with me and offered me an enormous amount of money--"

Ruth interrupted. "Forget all that. Tell us what you brought us out in the cold to say."

Mr. Rutledge exhaled, sending forth a puff of steam into the cold air. "Mrs. Higgins dictated this letter." He tapped the envelope against the arm of his rocking chair. "She said I should read it to you after she passed on." He put his briefcase beside his chair, took a long sheet of paper from the envelope, unfolded it, and read.

To Ruth Garland Jarrett:

If I intend to reach the pearly gates, I must make amends for a great injustice done by Eli, my husband of forty-two years. By hiding his evil deed, I became his accomplice. May God forgive me.

Eli is the man who attacked Faith Elizabeth Mackey. I know he is the culprit because I caught him in the very act.

George Mackey, Faith's father, is the overseer of Eli's farms. He has worked for Eli for many years. One afternoon George sent Faith to Eli's office to turn in his monthly reports. Eli took advantage of the girl then threatened her with dire consequences if she ever dared tell what he had done. I stood outside his office door and heard it all.

After Faith left his office in tears, I went inside and confronted him. He freely admitted what he had done. He then threatened to have me declared insane and send me to the state asylum, if I told. Eli is a powerful and vicious man. I knew he would make good on that threat. I kept his secret, but it ate at me like a cancer.

I am leaving the Higgins estate to Faith. I appoint Henry Jarrett as sole executor of my will. I know your reputation for honesty, Mr. Jarrett. I know you will see that she gets every cent of the money and properties left to her, and that you will protect her from those who would take it from her.

May God have mercy on my soul.
Arabella Collette Anson Higgins

Chapter Thirty-One

Cedar Gap, Texas
Tuesday Afternoon
January 14th, 1919

By mid-January Ruth and Henry decided it was safe to return home. Cases of flu had decreased considerably. Businesses, churches, and schools reopened. Henry opened his bank doors. Ruth stopped making daily rounds, but still spent a part of each weekday at the clinic.

Only after their return home did Henry tell Faith of her inheritance.

Faith's reaction when he told her the news of her good fortune was not what Ruth expected. The first words from her mouth were, "May I still work for you and Mrs. Jarrett?"

Ruth was stunned. "Why would you want to stay here when you have that huge mansion on Dove Street?"

Faith shuddered. "I will never enter that place again. Mr. Higgins has -- had -- his office in that house. Please let me stay here where I feel safe."

"Smoky Joe and his henchmen will never threaten you again," Henry assured her. "They are in prison and will be for a long time to come."

"I want to stay here and help care for Rosie, and Joe, and Jake. You won't have to pay me. I will pay you, if you let me stay."

The girl was still frightened. Ruth exchanged glances with Henry before she said, "Of course, you may stay. You don't need to pay us. You are well worth your keep."

Ruth was soon to learn why Faith was so afraid. It revealed itself when Faith's papa came to call. He talked of Faith's inheritance, and asked to speak to his daughter alone. There was no way Ruth was going to let that happen. "When," she held up one hand to silence her unwelcome visitor. "And if you speak to your daughter, it will be in my presence."

Mr. Mackey told Ruth, in no uncertain terms, that she had no part in this, and he intended to take control of Faith's estate and care for it and for his only child.

If he thought he could bully Ruth the way he had bullied his wife and daughter for all these years, he had better think again. She put a protective arm around Faith's quivering shoulders. "Like you 'took care of her' when she told you Eli Higgins molested her? You turned her out into the street. You are a poor excuse for a man. You are not worthy of the name papa."

Obviously no one had ever spoken to Mr. Mackey in such a manner. He opened his mouth and let go with a stream of denouncements and denials.

Halfway through his spiel, Henry came into the room. He said one word. "Enough."

Mr. Mackey stopped mid-sentence and spluttered, "I -- Faith -- who are you?"

Henry's voice was soft, smooth, and held a subtle warning. "I am the executor of Miss Mackey's estate. I have complete control over all her holdings. That includes the people she hires and fires. Mr. Mackey, you have ten days to vacate the house on your daughter's property. You will receive one month's severance pay. If you come near her-again, I will have you arrested and bring charges against you. Any jury that hears of your atrocious treatment of your wife and daughter, will find you guilty of any charges I choose to file."

"No," Faith cried. "He will hurt Mama."

"Your mama is safe," Ruth patted Faith's hand. "The moment your papa left his house his morning, Mr. Jarrett sent men to take her to a safe place."

Faith argued, "But Papa--"

"Will do nothing." Ruth completed Faith's sentence as she glared at Mr. Mackey. "Your papa is leaving Cedar Gap and he will never return. Mr. Jarrett has hired body guards to watch over your mama."

Like all bullies, Mr. Mackey was likewise a coward. He mumbled under his breath something about being blackmailed. His voice lifted as he declared aloud, "You can't scare me."

Henry grabbed the man by the collar. "Ruth, call the police. I suspect this man is guilty of stealing from the Higgins estate."

Mr. Mackey yanked himself free from Henry's grasp, and rushed toward the door. "You can't prove that."

"You are a wanted man," Henry said in a voice that demanded belief.

Mr. Mackey darted through the door and hurried down the sidewalk.

Henry watched his every move as he skulked toward his wagon. "He won't bother you again."

Faith pleated the hem of her handkerchief. "Are you sure?"

"I am very sure," Henry said.

Ruth echoed his words and added, "You never have to fear him again."

"I will buy a little house for Mama. She will love having a little place all her own. I still want to stay here and keep my nursemaid job. May I?"

Nothing would please Ruth more. She cast a questioning glance in

Henry's direction.

Henry smiled, first at Ruth, then at Faith. "Of course you may stay."

Later that evening, for the first time in months, Ruth and Henry had their evening time together in the closed quarters of Henry's office.

Henry sat in the chair behind his desk. "Privacy is a luxury I never appreciated until I no longer had it. God grant that my wife and I are never again forced to live in cramped quarters with three extra people." His smile melted Ruth's heart. "Speaking of God, I will confess publicly my acceptance of Jesus as my savior when we attend church services Sunday morning."

How many times had Ruth dreamed of her husband sitting beside her and the children, worshiping in the House of God? She returned his smile. "You are no longer an agnostic?"

"Never," Henry replied. "I believed before the flu epidemic. Suffering through it has reinforced my faith, and strengthened my admiration for you. You are the strongest, most compassionate woman I have ever known."

Such high praise. Ruth was both humbled and proud. "Through this troubled period my appreciation of you, and love for you have grown stronger and deeper. Now we can look forward to a future together.

"Do you have some specific plans?" Henry asked.

Ruth definitely did. "I would like to buy a piano and find a music teacher for Rosie. She loves music and she was fascinated by the piano in the hotel in Hallettsville."

Henry nodded his approval. "That's an excellent idea." He shifted in his chair. "I am thinking Jason would make an excellent replacement for Faith's papa. He will make a good overseer. He knows about farming, and he's honest. Shall I speak to him about it?"

This time it was Ruth who nodded her approval. "That's an excellent idea."

Henry came from behind his desk, and extended his hand in her direction.

Ruth stood and took his hand. "I love you, Henry Jarrett."

Henry pulled her near and held her close. "I love you, Ruth Jarrett. Come with me and I will show you how much."

*****

Cedar Gap, Texas
Sunday Morning
January 19th, 1919

Ruth had never been more proud. Her family, which now included Mrs. Murphy and Faith, filled half a pew. *This is the way God meant it to be.*

Pastor Cooper took his sermon text from *Jeremiah 18: 3-4.* Opening his Bible, he read:

> *Then I went down to the potter's house, and, behold he wrought a work on the wheels. And the vessel that he made of clay was marred in the hand of the potter: so he made it again another vessel, as seemed good to the potter to make it. KJV*

He closed his Bible, and looked out over the congregation. "My friends, we have, as a church, and as a community, come through a time of trial and testing. As a group we have suffered tremendous loss. Individually each of us has lost friends and loved ones. Some might argue this is a punishment from Almighty God. I am persuaded our Heavenly Father is only making us into more perfect vessels, better fitted to serve Him."

He stepped to the side of his pulpit, and paused a moment before speaking again. "Being a Christian does not guarantee sunny skies and tranquility. Quite often the opposite is true. When trials and tribulations come into our lives, it is the pressure of the potter's hand, shaping us into a more perfect vessel. If we struggle and resist, or become hostile and angry, He will crush us into a lump once more, and begin, again, to shape us into a more perfect receptacle. I pray you don't let your human will mar the excellence of God's creation."

Pastor Cooper stepped back behind his pulpit, and grasped its sides. "Jeremiah learned an important lesson that day long ago when he visited the potter's house. This lesson was, a Supreme God controls our lives. God is the potter. We are the clay. If we accept the workings of the potter, He will complete the work He has begun in us."

He released the sides of his podium, stepped to one side, and extended his hands in a pleading gesture. "The same God who molds and remolds Christians' lives, sent His only son Jesus to die for the sins of us all. If you do not know this Jesus as your personal savior, step forward as we sing a hymn of invitation, and accept Him. Even through sufferings and misfortunes, He will stand by you and put peace in your heart."

The moment the first chord of music burst forth, Henry moved to the aisle and walked toward Pastor Cooper.

Ruth bowed her head. "Thank you, Jesus."

Chapter Thirty-Two

Cedar Gap, Texas
Sunday Evening
January 19th, 1919

That evening at dinner, Ruth looked at the people sitting around the table, and silently thanked God for her many blessings.

Henry helped himself to a second serving of roast beef. "Pastor Cooper preached a fine sermon this morning."

Joe reached for his serving of bread pudding. "I didn't understand it."

For once Jake agreed with his brother. "Neither did I."

"I did," Rosie said. "It's like when our heavenly mama died. I asked God why so many times. He never told me. Now I know He had a reason, even though He never saw fit to tell me what it was."

Jake's bottom lip shaped into a pout. "What reason?"

Rosie shook her head. "I don't know that. Maybe God doesn't want me to know. Maybe He wants me to accept His will, trust Him and go on serving Him."

Faith touched her napkin to her lips. "You are a smart girl, Rosie, to learn that while you are young. God had to take my baby girl from me before I learned to accept and trust Him in all circumstances."

Mrs. Murphy spoke. "I was much older that you were, Faith, when I learned that hard lesson. It came when Oscar, my husband, passed away."

Ruth had never stopped asking why. She must strive to never make that mistake again. From this day forward, she would ask for grace to accept what came, as God's will, and not question why.

Henry pushed his chair back. "I am fortunate to be surrounded by Christians who have experience. I am so new at being God's child." He stood. "If you will excuse me, I have work to do."

Ruth laid her knife and fork across her plate. "Rosie, you are a very perceptive young lady." *Someday Rosie would attend college, and no doubt, graduate at the head of her class.*

Jake put his elbows on the table and rested his face in his hands. "What about me. Am I prospective too?"

Ruth laughed. "I would say so, yes. Come along the three of you. It's time to get ready for bed."

Faith jumped to her feet. "Do you want me to put them to bed, Mrs. Jarrett?"

"No. I will do it tonight." Ruth wanted some time alone with her children.

Later, when Ruth and Henry were in their bedroom, Henry asked, "Shouldn't we have a prayer time before we retire?"

Ruth's heart rejoiced. She entertained the same thought. She was reluctant to mention the subject. Henry would find his way to a closeness to God without her pushing him. "I would love that."

They knelt facing each other. Henry took both her hands, and bowed his head.

"I am so blessed to come to you, dear God, and to know that now you are my Heavenly Father. I thank you for the many blessings you have poured out on me. I want to serve you. Show me the way. Thank you for my dear wife and my sweet children, and for Faith, and Mrs. Murphy. I ask my prayer in the blessed name of my Lord and Savior, Jesus Christ. Amen."

Tears clogged Ruth's throat and fell from her eyes as she prayed, "Heavenly Father, thank you for your many blessings. Thank you for my dear husband and my precious children. Thank you for sending Mrs. Murphy and Faith to be a part of my family. Help me to no longer ask why. Help me to accept your will and serve you--" Emotion overtook her as a sob tore from her throat.

"Amen," Henry said as he pulled his wife into his arms and smoothed her hair. "Don't cry, my darling."

"I can't -- *sob* -- help it." Ruth buried her face in Henry's shoulder. "I'm so happy."

Henry stood and pulled her to her feet. He took a handkerchief from his pocket and dried her tears. "It's time we dressed for bed, happy girl."

Ruth smiled through her tears. "I love you, Henry Jarrett."

"And I--" Henry began.

He was interrupted by a loud bang on the door, and the twins calling out in unison, "Come in a hurry, Aunt Mama. Rosie is sick."

Henry raced to the door and flung it open. "What's wrong with Rosie?"

Jake's eyes were wide with alarm. "She's throwing up all over everything."

Terror riveted Ruth to the spot where she stood. *Not the flu, dear Lord. Please, not the flu.* "It must be something she ate." Her gaze met Henry's. She read in his eyes the same fear that gripped her. She motioned for the twins to come into the room. "Stay here with Papa. I will go to Rosie."

Henry laid a hand on her arm. "Wear a face mask."

Ruth called as she raced down the hall. "I will." She was rummaging in a hall chest of drawer for a mask when, from nowhere, Mrs. Murphy appeared.

"What are you looking to find?"

Ruth was beside herself with worry and fear. "I need a face mask. I remember putting some in here."

"They are in the second drawer," Mrs. Murphy said. Then she asked. "Why do you need a face mask?"

Ruth opened the second drawer. "Rosie is throwing-up. Henry says I should wear a face mask, just in case."

"Get two. You will need help."

Ruth couldn't let Mrs. Murphy expose herself to the flu. "I can manage alone."

"Shut up and get two masks."

Ruth obeyed and gave a mask to Mrs. Murphy. Her brave façade crumbled. "I hope and pray she doesn't have the flu." She grabbed Mrs. Murphy's hand. "I'm scared."

Mrs. Murphy pulled her hand from Ruth's grasp and put on her mask. "We're both scared. Let's go."

Ruth paused at the bottom of the staircase. "There is no point in you exposing yourself to a deadly--"

Mrs. Murphy was halfway up the stairs. She looked back over her shoulder. "Will you stop arguing and start moving? Rosie needs us."

Ruth lifted her skirt and followed Mrs. Murphy up the stairs, down the hall, and into Rosie's room.

Once inside, the sight that met Ruth's eyes, terrified her. Rosie lay in a pool of vile vomit. Its dreadful odor permeated the room. Rosie's long, lovely hair was drenched in the sticky stuff.

Mrs. Murphy moved to the other side of Rosie's bed. "Lift up the child. I will change the bedding and we can get her out of these clothes."

Her words galvanized Ruth to action. She lifted Rosie in her arms.

Mrs. Murphy stripped the bed, and fetched clean sheets and pillow slips.

Ruth sat in a chair and hugged Rosie to her. It was like caressing a flame. The child had a raging fever.

Rosie opened her eyes and looked up into Ruth's face. "Aunt Mama, I'm sick, really sick."

Her words were a dagger through Ruth's heart. "Mrs. Murphy and I will get you cleaned up. You will feel better when you are nice and clean and in an unsoiled bed.

Rosie closed her eyes. "I stink. My hair stinks. Will you wash it?"

An ominous sensation traveled down Ruth's spine and lodged in the pit of her stomach, forcing her to face an irrefutable truth. Rosie had the flu. The chances of her surviving the ordeal that lay ahead were slim to none. *Please, dear Heavenly Father, let her survive.*

"Washing your hair now is not a good idea. I will trim the vomit spots away." She would have to cut away most of Rosie's lovely curls. At this moment cleanliness was more important than curls. "Are you okay with that?"

Rosie nodded her consent. Ruth doubted she was coherent enough to know what she was agreeing to.

Mrs. Murphy brought warm water with disinfectant added, fresh underwear, and a clean nightgown.

Carefully, gently, and lovingly Ruth stripped and washed Rosie before dressing her in her clean clothes. The child clung to Ruth, "Promise me you won't go away. Stay with me."

Ruth's heart shattered. "I'm here, baby, and I will stay here."

Mrs. Murphy approached carrying a large pair of scissors. "Lift her hair. I will do the cutting."

This was a woman Ruth had once come close to hating. How wrongly she had judged Mrs. Murphy's actions. She lifted Rosie's mane of hair and Mrs. Murphy cut it and dropped it onto a soiled pillow slip.

Ruth covered Rosie with a blanket Mrs. Murphy brought. "Be sure you burn the pillow slip along with the hair in an outside receptacle."

A rigorous chill ran through Rosie's body.

Ruth held her closer. "It's okay, baby, don't be afraid."

Rosie clutched Ruth's dress front. "Don't leave me."

"I'm here for as long as you want me to stay." Ruth thought of the torturous hours ahead. She bowed her head and silently prayed, *Dear Jesus, you know about suffering. Comfort Rosie now in her hour of greatest need. Don't let her feel pain and don't let her die. Be merciful to her.*

Mrs. Murphy knelt beside Ruth's chair and prayed, "Help Ruth, dear Lord, during the hours ahead. Give her strength and assurance of your presence. Please, Lord. Don't take Rosie from us." She stood and wiped her eyes with her apron tail. "I am going downstairs. Mr. Jarrett will be up soon. I will be with him. Faith can mind the twins."

Ruth nodded. "Come back soon."

Chapter Thirty-Three

Cedar Gap, Texas
Monday Morning
January 20th, 1919

A string of mares' tail clouds floated across the horizon as a gray dawn broke across the eastern sky. Mrs. Murphy went downstairs to make a pot of coffee.

Henry sat in the chair Ruth had occupied most of the night. He held Rosie in his arms. Around four o'clock the child's skin took on a bluish hue. Now dark brown spots appeared on her cheeks. Chills and fever shook through her body. Sporadically she was racked with a spasm of coughing.

Ruth sat on Rosie's bed. She had seen these debilitating symptoms so many times before. She knew what they foretold. "I should be holding her. I promised I would stay with her." Through a long and terrifying night Ruth had begged God for mercy, and clung tenaciously to hope. "Pray with me, Henry. Beg God not to take our little girl."

Henry's haggard face reflected despairing weariness. He bowed his head. "Dear Heavenly Father, hear our prayer and heal Rosie if that be your will. Amen."

Ruth stood and held out her arms. "Let me hold my baby girl."

"You have held Rosie most of the night," Henry replied. "Mrs. Murphy will return soon with coffee. Drink a cup and then we will discuss you holding Rosie for a while."

Ruth refused to move. "Please, Henry, let me hold my little girl."

A fit of coughing tortured Rosie's small body. Henry hugged her closer until it passed.

Time was growing short. Unless God sent a miracle, Rosie would not see another dawn. "*Please,* Henry."

Henry stood and stepped aside.

Ruth sat in the chair and held out her arms.

Henry put Rosie in her lap.

Ruth held the child's fever-racked body close to her heart. "Sweet little girl, don't leave us now. I have such plans for you. Papa and I are going to buy a piano especially for you. Did you know that? You are going to grow up in a loving home, with a real family and toys, and pretty clothes -- all the things that make a little girl happy. You will never have to hide from your papa because he comes home roaring drunk, or have a mama that tells you what a disappointment you are to her; or wear hand-me-down clothes, or cry because other children call you elephant, or hippo, or ugly." Tears flowed from Ruth's eyes and ran down her cheeks. She lifted her head toward heaven. "Please, God, *no*."

Mrs. Murphy returned with a carafe of coffee and three cups. "We can all use something warm inside us." She poured coffee into the cups and gave one to Henry.

Rosie made a rattling sound deep in her throat as a sudden gush and blood and phlegm spurted from her mouth. She went limp in Ruth's arms.

"No!' Ruth screamed. "Please, God, no!"

Henry gave Mrs. Murphy his half-empty cup, took the child from Ruth's arms and laid her on her bed. "She's gone."

Grief swamped Ruth. She screamed, "Bring her back, Lord. Please, bring her back."

Henry's voice cracked. "Ruth, you are asking for the impossible."

Ruth looked heavenward. "I am not. Christ raised Lazarus from the dead. Why not Rosie?"

Henry pulled Ruth to her feet and gathered her in his arms. She looked up into his grief-stricken face. "Why, Henry, why?"

Henry held her close. He couldn't keep the anguish from his voice. "I don't know the answer to that. Maybe it's like Rosie said last night at dinner. 'Maybe God doesn't want me to know. Maybe he wants me to accept His will, trust Him and go on serving Him'."

Ruth closed her eyes and dropped her chin against a sudden surge of pain. Her resolve not to question God's will had vanished, swept away in a tidal wave of loss and misery. "Forgive me, Jesus. Take away my doubt." Rosie understood what Ruth found so difficult to grasp and accept. "Not my will but Thine."

Mrs. Murphy wept openly. "Ruth, do you recall what King David said when his son died? 'He cannot return to me, but I can go to him.' Some day we will see Rosie again. Meanwhile, you have two sons who need you. They *don't* need to see you in tears. Go to them, comfort them, and stop questioning God's will for us all."

Two years ago Ruth would have thought those words harsh and unfeeling. Today she knew they came from a heart filled with love. She dried her tears. "You are right. Was there ever a time you weren't?"

Mrs. Murphy actually smiled. "It's doubtful." She addressed Henry, "Take Mrs. Jarrett downstairs. I will attend to--" She paused and wiped her nose on the tail of her apron. "I will take care of things here."

Henry took Ruth's hand in his and they walked down the hall toward the staircase. Ruth felt the presence of The Holy Spirit. Her abysmal sorrow was made bearable by knowing the sweet peace of God's love.

Henry squeezed her hand. "Thank you, Ruth, for leading me to know Jesus as my savior. Without the knowledge of His saving grace, I would not be assured that Rosie is secure in His loving arms."

Ruth returned his squeeze. "With His help, we will get through this."

They turned the corner and looked down to see Faith and the twins standing at the foot of the stairs.

Faith took one look at them standing there, looking down at her, and stepped behind Jake and Joe. Tears filled her eyes and her face contorted in grief.

Jake and Joe's questioning faces were turned upward. Jake asked, "Is Rosie okay?" Joe echoed his query, "Yeah, is Rosie okay?"

Faith put one arm around each boy's shoulder. "Let's go into the kitchen. I will make breakfast. Your mama and papa will talk to you there."

To Ruth's surprise they went without questions or argument. She held onto Henry's hand as they descended. "How can we tell them Rosie is gone and she is not coming back?"

Henry swallowed. "God will help us know what to say."

His faith touched Ruth. Never before had she felt so strongly the shallowness of her own Christian walk. They were halfway down the stairs, when she paused. "We must take off these contaminated clothes and clean in disinfectant."

As if she had been given a cue, Faith reappeared at the bottom of the stairs. "I prepared a tub on the screen porch and laid out clean clothes for both of you. I was going to make a place in the bathroom. Mrs. Murphy said there was no point spreading germs all through the house. I put the canvas curtains down. I hope you don't freeze."

Henry thanked Faith as he guided Ruth toward the screened porch.

Like so many times before, Ruth and Henry went through the ritual of cleaning their bodies and changing their clothing.

As Ruth buttoned the front of her dress, words from Pastor Cooper's Sunday sermon paraded through her mind. *Some might argue this is a punishment from Almighty God. I am persuaded our Heavenly Father is only making us into more perfect vessels, better fitted to serve Him.* She clung to those words. They were the sustaining buoy that kept her from sinking in a sea of grief.

Henry completed his task, and knelt on the cold, hard floor. "Pray with me, Ruth. Help me get through what has happened, and what lies ahead."

Ruth knelt beside her husband. *Henry is asking me to help him. Doesn't he know how weak and needy I am? Who will help me?*

An inaudible voice spoke to her heart. *I will help you, my daughter. I will never leave you nor forsake you.* She had prayed so many times to God, but she had never before thought of Him as her Father. He *was* her Father, her Heavenly Father. She had a father who cared.

The revelation came swiftly. She must be strong. Rosie was with

Jesus and Rachel. Henry, Joe, and Jake were here with her. They needed her. She took Henry's hand and bowed her head. "Dear Heavenly Father..."

Chapter Thirty-Four

Cedar Gap, Texas
Sunday Morning
April 20th, 1919

Ruth sat in the auditorium of the church. Henry sat to her right. The twins were on her left, first Jake, then Joe. Beyond Joe, Mrs. Murphy and then Faith each occupied a seat. Jason sat on the far side of Faith. What was he doing here? He didn't believe in attending church. Was he trying to curry favor with his new employer? She discarded that thought. Stooping to deception to make points with his boss was not Jason's way.

Who was she to judge? For three months she had been living a lie, travelling along, going through her empty daily routine. All the while she was vacant inside. At one time she had such high hopes of serving God in some place where she was needed. She knew Henry and the boys needed her, but that need didn't fill a huge gap in her life, the challenge to serve God, to reach out to others with His message of hope and salvation. She was like a ship without a rudder, drifting away from the shore.

A ragamuffin child burst through the back door of the church, shouting as he stopped just inside the entrance, "Nurse woman, help me. Papa is bleeding something awful."

Ruth recognized the boy. His name was Moses Welch. His family lived in a tent near the forks of the river. They cut and sold wood for a living. She stepped around Henry and ran toward the child. "Where is your papa?"

Moses opened the door and rushed down the steps. "Out here, in the wagon."

The man in the wagon gritted his teeth. "My axe flew off the handle," he explained, as Ruth crawled into the wagon and examined a long gash along the upper part of his left leg.

She raised her dress, ripped off the ruffle of her petticoat, and made a bandage.

A gaunt, stern-faced woman sat on the seat of the wagon. "We couldn't find the doctor. Nobody knows where he is."

Ruth pressed the blood-soaked bandage over the open wound. "Do you know the way to the clinic?" She hadn't been to the clinic since Rosie's death.

Henry jumped into the wagon seat and took the reins. "We're on our way."

Over the next hour Ruth cleaned and stitched Mr. Welch's wound. The cut was long, but not deep. The wound would heal without permanent damage to his leg.

Through the entire procedure, Henry was by her side, assisting as only he could. He sighed as she completed her work, and smiled at her. "We can go now and tell the patient's family the good news."

Ruth wiped her hand across her brow. "He will sleep for a while." She covered Mr. Welch with a light blanket.

The moment they came into the clinic's waiting area, Mrs. Welch jumped to her feet and ran toward them. "Is Emmett going to be all right?"

Moses asked, "Can we see Papa now?"

"Yes, your husband will be all right," Ruth told Mrs. Welch. "He must stay off his feet for a few weeks." She smiled down into the boy's anxious face. "Your papa is asleep now. You can see him when he is awake."

"You saved his life," Mrs. Welch wiped at her tears, moved back to her chair and sat down. "Thank you, Jesus, for hearing and answering my prayer."

Ruth sat beside the woman. "What did you pray for, Mrs. Welch?"

"First I prayed we would get to the doctor in time. I was scared Emmett would bleed to death. When I knew the doctor couldn't be found, I prayed there would be someone around who knew how to help him. Then Moses remembered how his friend, Aaron Crawford had told him about a nurse in town, and how that nurse saved his mama and his baby brother's life. I prayed I would find you, and I did, in church."

In that revealing instant, Ruth knew where God had wanted her to serve Him all along. The disclosure had not come to her sooner because she was not a fit vessel to serve Him. First He must mold her and then make her, and then break her and reshape her, creating a vessel fit for His service. Four years of study gave her the knowledge for her mission. What she lacked was the compassion for those who suffered, and the dedication to God's high calling. She bowed her head. "Thank you, Jesus." Her brain was teeming with plans and her heart was thankful. She turned to Henry. "I have found my calling. I was in the right place all along."

Henry smiled at her and sweet peace filled her soul. "I know, my dear. I have known since I jumped into the Welch's wagon and took the reins."

How well he knew her. How much she loved him. "We have so many plans to make."

"Later." Henry said. "Now I must go home. Mrs. Murphy, Joe, Jake, Faith, and Jason are waiting for me."

Ruth remembered something she should have recalled much earlier. "Faith and Jason were to have Sunday dinner with us. Faith says she has an important announcement to make to the family."

Henry nodded. "I know. Jason talked to me earlier. We will all be there when you get home." Without waiting for an answer, he was out the door and gone.

Ruth turned her thoughts to the pressing matter of her patient and his family. She returned to sit, once more beside Mrs. Welch. "You and I have many things to discuss."

*****

It was after three o'clock before Ruth reached home. She was scarcely through the front door when Joe and Jake raced to her shouting, "Guess what." Before she could answer, Jake announced in a loud voice that bounced around the room. "Faith and Jason are going to be married."

Henry followed them. "Your sons can't keep a secret."

Faith and Jason came into the room. They were arm-in-arm. Faith's face glowed with happiness. Jason was all smiles. "I wanted to tell you myself," Faith said, "but it seems the cat is already out of the bag."

Joe tugged Ruth's skirt. "Faith is going to be Leon's new mama."

Mrs. Murphy appeared in the doorway. "Ruth, if you don't want to eat a cold meal, get to the table."

The group in front of her moved aside and Ruth came into the dining room and sat down.

Mrs. Murphy sat a plate in front of her. Ruth picked up her knife and fork. "This roast beef looks delicious." She was ravenous.

As the others settled around the table, Jason asked, "How is your patient?"

Ruth swallowed before saying. "He's going to be all right. I told the Welches to stay at the clinic tonight. I hate the thought of that poor man trying to stay warm and pain-free in a tent during this kind of weather."

Faith caught Jason's hand, pulled him nearer, and whispered in his ear.

A smile spread across Jason's face. "Of course it's all right. It's more than all right."

Faith gave Jason a nudge. "You tell them."

Jason stood. "Faith wants to give the house on Dove Street, the one that once belonged to Mr. and Mrs. Higgins, to you, Ruth, to use as a place for homeless and needy people, like the Welches."

That home was in the most elite section of Cedar Gap. Ruth could imagine what the neighbors would say about such an arrangement. "I'm not sure the city would approve. I know nearby residents wouldn't."

"I have a suggestion." Henry said. Heads swiveled to look in his direction. "You can sell the house and establish a foundation. The interest from the money of the sale of the house will go a long way toward funding the clinic."

Faith clapped her hands. "Yes, do that."

Ruth forgot the sadness of the past few months. She had a mission. Its accomplishment depended on Mrs. Murphy's help. "There is one other problem that must be addressed. I need your commitment to our cause, Mrs. Murphy."

Mrs. Murphy opened her mouth to speak.

Ruth raised a silencing hand. "Wait, hear what I have to say. As badly as I want to open and run a free clinic in Cedar Gap, I can't do it if it means neglecting Joe and Jake, and my home. There is only one person I trust to take my place while I am away, and that person is you. You don't have to answer now. You can think about it for a while, if you feel the need to do that."

Henry broke into the conversation. "I will hire a couple of people to help you with the heavy work, but I do hope you will continue to do the cooking. No one can best your culinary abilities."

He spoke as if this was a done deal. Ruth didn't want him to assume too much.

Mrs. Murphy said, "I will."

Ruth breathed an audible sigh of relief. "You will need to move your bedroom upstairs to be near Jake and Joe."

Mrs. Murphy stood and began to stack dishes. "You run your clinic. I will take care of things here."

Ruth wanted to laugh. She stifled her giggle. She didn't want to chance that Mrs. Murphy might still change her mind.

Not so for Henry. He burst into a belly laugh. When he could control his guffaws, he said. "That, Mrs. Jarrett, should put you in your place."

Ruth released her giggle. "Well said, Mr. Jarrett." She smiled into her husband's loving eyes.

From her turmoil, God gave her peace. From her grief, He showed the way to service. From her doubt, He gave her knowledge.

In the day of prosperity be joyful, but in the day of adversity consider: God also hath set the one over against the other, to the end that man should find nothing after him. Ecclesiastes 7:14 KJV

The End

54697531R00089

Made in the USA
Charleston, SC
12 April 2016